Avery Balthazar is having the worst. Christmas. Ever! Just that morning, she was standing in the corporate headquarters of Balthazar Broadcasting, her stepfather's mega-media empire situated in downtown Manhattan. But after a brief trip across the country in the company Learjet, she is suddenly standing face to face with her high school crush, Branch Asher. What's worse, she has the unenviable task of buying out his own mini empire on behalf of her family business, when the only "business" she's really interested in is getting Branch into bed, once and for all!

Branch Asher is having the best. Christmas. Ever! He's got his old high school crush, Avery Balthazar, right where he wants her: back in their old hometown of Lakemont, California for three whole days until she gives her pitch to buy his company, which he's in no hurry to sell. The only thing Branch is in a hurry to do this Christmas, after all, is to tempt Avery into living out a few of his old high school desires, one illicit fantasy at a time!

A Very Merry Merger
Copyright © 2022 Alex Winters
ISBN: 978-1-4874-3686-5
Cover art by Angela Waters

Published by eXtasy Books Inc

Look for us online at,
www.eXtasybooks.com

A Very Merry Merger
An Erotic Holiday Novel

By

Alex Winters

CHAPTER ONE: AVERY

"And just how do you think that went, dear?"

Avery Balthazar glanced across the lavish boardroom atop the family's massive corporate headquarters in downtown Manhattan. There were leather chairs left askew, papers scattered, and water bottles empty atop the gleaming cherry wood conference table.

Her sigh was as heavy as her recently embattled heart. "Well, no one quit, Dad, so . . . there's that."

Her stepfather's voice was low and unmistakably ominous. "They might not have resigned from the organization, dear, but I would wager a significant percentage quit supporting you as a leader just now, Avery."

She regarded her stepfather, every prematurely silver hair in place to match his world-weary meaningless grin. Inside his exquisitely tailored three-piece suit, Avery knew he was quietly, even patiently, seething. She leaned back against the bamboo wall covering and peered past the man seated at the head of the table to the framed portrait of the same man sitting in the same chair right overhead.

It often struck Avery what a wild, strange ride it had been to become part of this storied, rich, and famous man's family, and how much she simply didn't belong in that same chair, her portrait next to his on that same wall.

No matter how much he tried to will it into being.

"Did they ever?" She huffed, aching to kick off her heels and have a massive mango-rita at Salsa Sally's Mexican Cantina around the corner from Balthazar Broadcasting HQ.

"They might have, dear, if you'd given them half a chance today."

"It's curious to me, Father, how you can say that on the very day you made me the head of Themed Eateries and Entertainment." She waved an arm around the now empty boardroom, practically seething and contemptuous only minutes earlier. "I mean, wasn't that what today's little meeting was all about? To introduce me and put to bed all the rumors?"

Archibald Marigold Balthazar, founder and CEO of Balthazar Broadcasting, gave her a wry, humorless grin. "I thought that's what I *was* doing, dear. After all, it's tradition to give the boss's son a promotion upon graduation." His eyes scoured her curiously. Never one to wear his emotions on his sleeve, her adoptive father constantly kept her on guard. She wondered, idly, if that was his intent. "Or, in this case, the boss's daughter."

"Stepdaughter," she reminded him for perhaps the millionth time.

"That's . . . not how I think of you, Avery. Nor has it ever been."

"Nor I, you, Archibald. But it's what all those other department heads in that meeting just now think, and we have to face facts someday."

"Facts such as?"

"That very few of them want me to be your successor as much as, say, they might have, had you sired an actual son."

"But I didn't, dear. I have you, Avery. And you are the person I put in charge of this company's latest division. Period."

Avery nodded, her half-smile fixed despite the raging tension headache roaring behind her ears. "And as such, Father, I merely held my ground while the head of every other division in your company second-guessed, groaned, and disparaged every other word of my plans for the next quarter."

The old man nodded. "Perhaps that's because your plans were so . . . esoteric."

"Can you blame me, Dad? I mean, Themed Eateries and Entertainment? What even *is* that?"

He gave her a wry, unaccustomed smile. He was, as ever, clearly enjoying her obvious displeasure. "Why, it's a brand-new division, dear, one designed to tie all of our other divisions—radio, TV, filmed entertainment, internet, podcasts, social media—together through, well . . . Themed Eateries and Entertainment."

She threw up her hands. "No one knows what that is, Dad."

"And they won't, dear. At least, not until you show them the way. That's why I handed it to you, Avery. That's why, in essence, I created it for you. I want you to guide this company into the future, if you so desire. And to do that, you will have to learn what it's like to stand on your own two feet, no matter what your rivals may throw in your face."

"By guiding an empty division with nothing to fill it? No wonder the whole room was snickering behind my back today, Dad. Or, in many cases, straight to my face."

His eyes grew severe again, a clear signal she was veering off track and he was eager for her to rein herself in. "They were snickering because you showed no clear guidance, dear. That's what they were looking for from you today."

"It wouldn't have killed you to stick up for me, Dad," she said, relenting and unbuttoning the muted gray jacket of her new pantsuit, bought special for what Archibald kept referring to as her *coronation day.*

He nodded almost imperceptibly. "No, but it would have killed whatever legitimacy you might have gained for yourself up there today. Remember, Avery, this new division of Balthazar Broadcasting will sink or swim depending on you and you alone."

Her throat tightened with the sudden mantle of responsi- bility. "So you remind me every other minute since I gradu- ated last week, Dad."

Avery's father stood slowly and turned his back to her. She would have taken it personally had she not known that the cabinet behind his seat was where the old man hid his private stash. She was relieved when she heard the clink of telltale ice cubes hit the bottom of two rocks glasses, and not just his own. Four quick gurgles and he turned, offering an olive branch in the form of 40-year-old barreled bourbon from their private distillery nestled deep in the Kentucky foothills.

"You've got to quit being so sensitive, dear," he urged, tap- ping her glass with his own in a casual, almost affectionate, way. "You're not an intern anymore, remember? Or a gradu- ate student, for that matter. You're here, in the room, at the table . . ." He waved his glass at the empty conference room before taking a long, healthy quaff of his favorite whiskey. "You don't need to waste another word defending yourself."

"Well, someone has to." She huffed before taking a sip and letting the warm, whiskey tones sear the emotions gurgling in the back of her throat.

He scoffed with a quick shake of his head. "You confuse my silence with agreement, Avery."

She clucked her tongue, waving her glass at the same empty table. "So do your lackeys, Dad. That's the point."

Her father rolled his soft blue eyes. "And you confuse words with admiration, Avery. You must earn their respect, and that's exactly what your first acquisition is going to do."

Avery felt the first prickle of apprehension sting the back of her neck, much the same way the bourbon had stung the back of her throat. "Acquisition?"

He slid a file folder across the table at her. It glided effort- lessly across the immaculately polished surface. She took an- other sip of bourbon and sank into the nearest chair, tapping it cautiously.

"What, pray-tell, is this?" Despite the question, Avery already knew it wouldn't be anything good.

"You're the new head of a new department, dear. But it hasn't turned a profit since we started it months ago, waiting for you to wrap up your MBA and join the company in your official status. You've already got a staff full of eager young employees, and a New Year's approaching with nothing to fill the upcoming calendar. What's in that folder, the name on that dossier, is going to change all that."

She glanced inside, read the name, and slammed it shut as if she might blot out her very own past. "Dad, honestly?"

"Who better to inaugurate your division than Branch Asher, dear?"

Suddenly, it all made sense. The new division. The sudden promotion. The corner office and willing, eager, young staff. Avery fixed her father with a withering glance. "So that's why you promoted me two days after graduation. And that's why you made me the head of a new division no one in this company has ever heard of yet. To snag Branch Asher as our very first get?"

He seemed more amused by her outburst than anything else. "You act like that's a bad thing, dear."

She picked up her glass and took a biting swig before waving it at him threateningly. And she noticed with some hint of surprise, emptily. "Bad isn't quite the word I'm thinking of, Father. Conniving, cunning, sneaky, low-down, those are some better ones."

The old man roared his approval, chuckling and snickering and slapping his hand on the table so that his *Harvard* class ring sang out with a silvery echo each time he did so. "I couldn't have said it better myself, Avery. But why the long face?"

"Dad, I just thought, after all these years, you might have

rewarded me based on merit, not . . . not . . . my social life. My former social life at that. I haven't seen Asher since . . . since high school graduation. That was nearly six years ago."

He stood abruptly, approaching her quickly despite the presence of his polished cane. A mild stroke several years earlier had robbed him of some of his mobility but not one ounce of his vitality.

"Avery, my dear, you simply *must* quit taking things so personally. This is business, and in business, the best leads are those we have a personal connection with. God knows I've taught you that much over the years."

"Dad, I sat behind him in homeroom. We hardly have a . . . connection."

"That's more than anyone else in this room has, Avery, and it's enough to get you in the door of Asher Enterprises, and hopefully, a seat at the bargaining table."

"Yeah," she mumbled to herself. "That's what I'm worried about."

He slapped her shoulder while belching out another thundering guffaw. She glanced up at him with something bordering affection. "I'm glad you're enjoying this, Father."

"Oh, I am, immensely, dear. And so will you if you'll just, excuse my French, take that stick out of your derriere and look at this as an opportunity."

"To what, Dad? Go back home and embarrass myself all over again?"

"I doubt anyone but Branch still lives in that dreary little one-horse town, dear. And besides, you have less than an hour to fret about it."

"How so?"

He dragged her from her perch with a surprisingly deft hand, shoving her toward the conference room door with another chuckling guffaw. "Because, Avery, your flight is precisely forty-seven minutes from now."

CHAPTER TWO: BRANCH

"**B**oss man?"

Branch Asher turned, a gory action figure in hand, to greet Spike, the head of his New Opportunities Division. They both knew it was a glorified name for a *receptionist*, but Spike liked sitting at the front of the warehouse, surrounded by funky, retro wall art and colorful bean bag chairs, introducing new clients, interns, or employees to Branch throughout the day.

"Yes, Spike?"

Spike looked nothing like his name, but instead soft and doughy. An abashed smile pushed adorable dimples across his apple cheeks. He had a severe emo-black tuft of hair that often covered his round Harry Potter glasses completely. Fashion-wise, Spike favored Hawaiian shirts over thrift shop concert tees, khaki clam diggers, and, of course, tie-dye *Crocs*.

Branch growled and waved the bloody bendable cheerleader like a starting pistol. Around them, Asher Enterprises hummed with a dozen different projects all at once.

The open floor plan, featuring cubicles instead of offices and not a door in sight, fairly buzzed with a dozen different projects merging all at once. His eager staff of devoted, creative, and mostly young employees — despite being only a few years older than most of them, Branch referred to them as *the Kids* — were laser-focused on whatever it was they had in their sights that day.

It could be redesigning an old menu for one of his new themed restaurants. It could be whipping up a quick recipe on one of his half-dozen foodie-related *YouTube* channels. It could be doing a video tour of his latest venture, a game room-slash-snack bar called Joystix. Whatever they were doing, whenever they were doing it, Branch liked to be only a few feet away if they had a question or, more than likely, a helpful suggestion.

"You have a walk-in appointment I think you're going to want to take." Behind his thick, round glasses, Spike gave Branch a little wink-wink, nudge-nudge action.

"Who is it, anyway?" he asked, ignoring Spike and returning to admiring his action figure, the carefully detailed mockup of a new toy for the gift shop of his horror-themed ice cream parlor, Scoops 'N Screams.

Spike glanced at the pink message form in his hand, squinting even with his thick glasses. "It's the representative from Balthazar Broadcasting, sir."

"What, again? I thought I ghosted them weeks ago."

"You did," came a familiar voice from behind Spike, making Branch grip the action figure as if his very life depended on it. "That's why I decided to come and pitch you personally, Branch."

"Avery?" Struggling not to stammer out her name, Branch could literally hardly believe his eyes. Like a schoolboy, he gulped and felt his palms instantly go clammy.

His throat constricted so that he could barely squawk, "Avery Balthazar?"

From the sidelines, Spike watched the exchange with supreme, unmitigated glee. All that was missing was his feet up on some nearby cushion and a bag of popcorn in his lap, eagerly enjoying the drama as if from some cut-rate soap opera.

Avery was, as ever, cool as a cucumber and all legs. "Who'd you think they'd send, Branch? The old man?"

Somehow, he managed to give his old high school crush an unwavering frown without actually falling over from shock and awe. "I wouldn't mind him seeing what we're doing here now, Avery. He never did think I'd amount to much."

Avery inched closer, a sleek leather valise slung over one shoulder of her tailored pantsuit jacket. She sure had come a long way since her rebellious teenage years and her standard uniform of short gingham skirts, punk rock t-shirts, and sleeveless denim jackets full of famous monster pins. To say nothing of those sexy fishnet stockings that she wore with her big, bulky black boots.

Branch had always wondered what she might look like without all of her emotional armor and often fantasized about peeling off each item, piece by piece. He knew she'd been groomed to work with her father since her teen years, but he'd never quite imagined what she'd look like in a corporate setting. He should have known she'd look much the same, no matter what she wore. Even in her fitted pantsuit and binding jacket, Avery couldn't hide the radiant, glowing sexuality and ripe, limber limbs that lurked just beneath the surface of all that Fifth Avenue fabric.

Her voice was low and somber, as if it hadn't been six years since they'd last seen each other. "He *has* seen what you're doing, Branch. That's . . . why I'm here."

Branch sank down onto the corner of his clear *Lucite* desk, cool teacher style, if only to keep his knees from knocking together in Avery's sudden, spectacular presence. All the same, business was business, and he'd tried to squelch Balthazar Broadcasting's efforts for months now.

Make that years.

His voice was a stiff, low simmer as he struggled to retain his composure and somehow resisting the urge to drink her body in, inch by inch, all the while. "If he's seen what I'm doing, Avery, then he should know I don't need his help."

Avery slipped the valise off her shoulder, sliding it onto a waist-high countertop just inside his cubicle. The motion was fluid, practiced, and vaguely irritating. He hadn't necessarily asked her to stay, and yet the subtle move was clearly intended to mark her territory, as it were. Spike noticed as well, giving Branch a *get-a-load-of-this* glance before he made his quick escape to the *Welcome Center* situated at the front of the warehouse proper.

Avery's tone, in reply, was equally demonstrative. "Perhaps *help* isn't the right word, Branch. Partner is more like it."

Branch nodded toward the beehive of activity beneath the warehouse roof. Podcasters, *TikTokers*, videographers, *YouTubers*, editors, and graphic designers all toiling under the Asher Enterprises banner of Themed Eateries and Entertainment. "Does it look like I need another partner, Avery?"

She followed his gaze, giving a curious nod to the hustle and bustle, the energy and the grind that was all part of Branch's mission to snap off his own private, lucrative corner of the themed nostalgia eatery wave he'd helped create.

Or, at the very least, reenergize.

When she glanced back at him, her eyes were as amused as the crooked grin on those ripe, full lips of hers. Jesus, Branch mused, struggling to keep his composure in her sudden presence. They were still just as kissable as ever.

"Looks like you could use a good babysitter, Branch. Are any of these kids over the age of sixteen?"

They agreed on that point, at least. "They are young, Avery, but that's what I like about them. They remind me of us when we were that age."

For the first time since she'd sauntered into his office, looking like she owned the damn place, Avery's carefully polished veneer cracked. Just a smidge.

"Us?"

"Sure," he reminded her, struggling to ignore the way Avery's pantsuit reminded him of those long coltish legs and how he'd stared at them in homeroom every morning, wondering what it might feel like to rub his fingertips up and down them, over and over again. "Remember that *YouTube* channel you started senior year called *Undercover Cafeteria*?"

She gave him a knowing smirk, another, albeit subtle, layer of her big city veneer gently slipping away beneath the warmth of that quick, semi-smile, and even quicker half-snort.

God, how he'd missed that snort.

"Now, how could I forget something like that?"

"But you did, didn't you?"

She sounded vaguely irritated, and even that sound he recalled fondly. Like her stepfather, Avery had always had a short fuse. "It . . . was some time ago, Branch."

He rolled his eyes. "Six years ago is hardly a lifetime, Avery. And not nearly long enough to forget the Great Food Fight of 4th Period Lunch!"

She chuckled in earnest, a hearty, husky, positively sexy sound as she rolled her eyes as if embarrassed that he'd finally gotten to her. "Okay, I'm not gonna lie. That . . . that was pretty good."

"Whatever happened to that channel anyway?"

She shrugged, struggling to regain her composure and not quite sealing the deal. "Dad made me take it down before I started applying to universities. Said it could adversely affect my chances of admission."

"Yeah, right. Like you weren't gonna get into the college of your choice no matter what, with Archibald Marigold Balthazar pulling the strings."

CHAPTER THREE: AVERY

"Are you . . . implying I didn't get into *Brown* on my own merits, Branch Asher?"

Avery enjoyed watching Branch squirm atop his modern-style desk, as long and limber and lean as he'd been the day she'd left him standing, slack-jawed and holding his black square cap, moments after graduation almost six years earlier.

"Hardly, I just . . ."

"Relax," she assured him, inching onto a stylish red barstool that matched the white plastic countertop where she'd rested her purse, if only to assure she had enough time to give him her pitch. Avery knew if she hurried, she could complete her carefully crafted speech before her palms grew too clammy, her knees started wobbling, and her voice started cracking.

But only if she started posthaste.

"I know what you meant, Branch. And sure, the old man may have pulled some strings, but the only school he ever *really* wanted me to attend was his alma mater, *Harvard*. Anything less than that was always going to be a bitter disappointment."

Their eyes met across the spacious cubicle, a sizzle of that old electricity charging the very air between them. *Jesus,* she realized, struggling not to drool at the sheer, utter radiance of Branch's casually beautiful face. *This is going to be a lot harder than I thought.*

"And now?" Branch asked, jutting his chin out at her in that cocky way of his.

She smirked, prodding herself with a confidence that she certainly didn't feel. At least, not sitting this close to Branch Frickin' Asher, of all people. "Now I'm the Head of Themed Eateries and Entertainment."

As if on cue, a bloodcurdling scream erupted from a nearby cubicle. Avery glanced over, a hand to her throat, wondering if she should call nine-one-one. A scene from a vaguely familiar-looking 80s horror movie played on a giant TV screen. In front of it, what looked to be two preteens wearing headphones murmured into fuzzy round microphones as they waved their hands mid-discussion.

"Sorry, the girls from the Gore Channel are live-tweeting *Biker Babes on Satan Street* to promote Scoops 'N Scares, and it gets a little loud when they start screaming."

"As Biker Babes are wont to do, naturally."

"Are you . . . being sarcastic right now?"

"Not really. I just . . ." Avery glanced at the bustling beehive of activity that was Asher Entertainment's thriving hub. Though the drab, tan warehouse had looked vaguely generic and ill-advised on the outside, inside it looked, sounded, and felt just like the creative mind that had created dozens of wildly popular themed eateries, shops, and other assorted entertainments in just a few short years. "This is quite the culture shock from standing atop Balthazar Broadcasting HQ just a few short hours ago."

Branch gave her a condescending *pffft* sound followed by a dismissive hand wave. "I can only imagine the stuffed shirts who work there."

She finally had the excuse to look him up and down, admiring every inch of his lean, sexy countenance. "You mean . . . like me?"

He returned the favor, his focus eagerly roving over her pressed suit, down to her statuesque heels, and back up again, lingering only momentarily on the soft chemise that hid her suddenly pounding chest.

"Present company excepted, of course."

She nodded. "Of course."

Avery glanced at several of the cubicles facing them. In each one, a different type of media was being explored by clearly energetic, hyper-focused, creative young people. One had a record player warbling a scratchy piece of vinyl while a girl in red pigtails videotaped it with her phone. Another had a drafting table featuring what looked to be pages of a colorful graphic novel. While another had the telltale recording booth vibe of a podcast.

"Are these . . . freelancers?"

Branch rolled his eyes. "Avery, these are all separate divisions of Asher Enterprises. Over there, you have folks creating the funky video feeds that play on the TVs in the background of my VHS rental store and snack bar, Rewind. Next to them are a couple of young graphic artists making original artwork for the walls of my Comic Book Café. Every person here has a purpose, and what's more, a passion. That's why I hire them. That's why I love being around them. They . . . inspire me."

Avery couldn't help but notice the zeal in Branch's eyes as he spoke of his various properties, to say nothing of his young employees. She wondered, idly, if her father had any inkling of how hard it was going to be to convince him to fold such an eclectic and clearly personal company into the Balthazar Broadcasting umbrella. She tried to keep her focus. After all, half of making an effective sales pitch was understanding the culture of the company in question.

"In . . . cubicles, though?"

Branch shrugged, eyeing her curiously. "I like the rhythm and flow of seeing what everyone's involved in at any given moment. It keeps me hustling. Closed doors and corner offices kind of defeat that particular purpose."

"So that's why your HQ is in a warehouse with an open floor plan?"

"It started as a workshare environment, mostly because the land was cheap, and constructing a warehouse was way faster than erecting a brand-new office building from scratch. But every time I'd walk by a new cubicle and see someone working on something, I just ended up investing in it. Now they're all full-fledged divisions and doing great things."

Avery saw her opportunity to broach the subject of why she and Branch were facing off in his poster-filled office in the middle of the day after having had zero contact for six whole years. "So, naturally, you think my company would be interfering."

"Duh?"

"Did . . . those folks across from us think you were interfering when you invested in them?"

Branch gave her a wagging finger in reply. "Is that what they taught you at *Brown*, Avery? Negotiating one-oh-one? Use the prospect's words against him?"

"Pretty sure my stepfather taught me that back in grade school, but . . . yeah, sure."

Branch beamed as if she hadn't just roasted him like an overdone rotisserie chicken. "Listen, this is all very interesting, and I'm glad you stopped by today. How long are you in town for?"

She squared up, tensing, the sound of a hasty kiss-off threatening in his tone. "That all depends on you, Branch."

Chapter Four: Branch

"Well, good. I hope you don't have any plans for Christmas."

Branch beamed. His mind was whirring, as it did when it seized on another golden opportunity. The woman of his dreams had just pranced into his office, and if there was one thing Branch knew, it was a good investment when he saw one.

No way was he letting this one get away so soon.

Meanwhile, Avery gave him a steely, knowing glance. Her severe tone matched the penetrating stare. "Of course I do, Branch. Of course we both do. And, of course, if you'll simply listen to my pitch today, it won't take anywhere near that long to seal this sweetheart of a deal." She tapped the sides of her monogrammed valise for emphasis, as if it, in fact, held such a deal inside.

He'd blurted the words out on pure instinct but realized that, for once, he held all the cards in this relationship. This was no longer nerdy Branch gazing at Avery from across the classroom, wistfully wishing he could work up the nerve to talk to her once and for all and day after day, failing miserably in that regard.

This time, for once, Avery truly and sincerely, almost desperately, wanted something he had, and it was the bargaining chip Branch had been dreaming of all his life. Suddenly playful, he looked forward to the next three days in a way he hadn't looked forward to anything in quite a long time.

Arms crossed over his chest, chin jutted out, and wearing

a giant, telltale smirk, Branch asked, "Did I say I wouldn't listen to your pitch, Avery?"

"You didn't say you would." She started to reach for her valise, and he waved his hands to stop her.

Amazingly, it worked. Another sign that, for once, the ball was in his court, and he had all the time in the world to play it cool, calm, and collected.

The reversal of fortune was as liberating as it was exciting.

"I said I wouldn't listen to your pitch *yet*, Avery Balthazar," he said, standing finally now that he'd acclimated to Avery's sensual, sudden presence and could trust himself not to get too *excited* about her arrival. "First, I get to give you mine."

She was suddenly skeptical, openly defiant, and flagrantly defensive. Branch loved every minute of it. "That's . . . not how this works."

"It does when you fly across the country and ambush me in my own corporate headquarters three days before Christmas, Avery." It felt strange saying that, to her of all people. In high school, Avery was the consummate "it" girl. Beautiful, popular, smart, sexy, sassy, aloof, she was literally out of reach for a guy like Branch. Suddenly, here she was, cold-calling his office to basically buy his company — and looking hotter than ever while doing it. Damn straight, he was going to do his best to string her along for as long as he could! And biding his time over the holiday weekend was just the ruse he needed to negotiate Avery Balthazar right into his bed.

Or, at the very least, die trying.

She rolled her eyes and clucked her tongue. "I'd hardly call it an ambush, Branch."

He waved another hand, as if trying to distract a wild animal from attack, then used it to grab her valise off the nearby countertop. "Hey!" Her face was a quick mix of frustration and curiosity. Even playfulness.

He held it gently out of reach. "Listen, you'll get to make

your precious pitch when I'm good and ready. Which should be, say, three days from now?"

Her eyes widened. Her hip cocked. Her lips pursed. "Branch Asher, if you think I'm sticking around crummy old Lakemont, California until Christmas Eve before you'll hear my pitch, you're crazier than I always knew you were."

He tapped his temple and winked, enjoying going toe-to-toe with a girl he'd never thought he'd see again in the first place. "Crazy built this empire, Avery. An empire you and your father want so badly you actually put on a damn three-piece suit and flew clear across the country to see me in, so . . ."

She tugged at her upturned collar, wearing a triumphant smile even though he was the one who'd just called her bluff. "Aw, you noticed."

"Sure, Avery," he said, gently steering her past the outer edge of his cubicle and out into the sprawling, frenetic hallway that ran the length of the warehouse. "I noticed you playing dress-up."

"This is how I dress now, Branch," she murmured, slinking along next to him on those endless, towering legs. Her stride was pure silk, her hips swaying gently from side to side, her upturned face a breath of fresh air after being absent so long. "So like it or lump it."

"Well, I hope you brought a change of clothes, sweetheart, because . . . you're going to need them if you're sticking around Lakemont for the holidays."

"I hadn't planned on it," she murmured as Branch continued moving her through a gaggle of rollerblading baristas delivering afternoon tea to the cubicles at his back. He couldn't help but notice the way they nearly dropped their recyclable cardboard trays giving Avery a second, then a third, glance as they careened past.

Branch was no priest, but he was a big believer in

separating church and state, and as such, rarely mixed business with pleasure. In fact, he couldn't remember the last time he'd brought one of his lovers to see the warehouse. To say nothing of a woman who looked, acted, and flat-out sauntered the way Avery Balthazar did.

"You're in luck." Branch beamed as he prodded her into a small kiosk located just off the warehouse's funky front entrance. "It's t-shirt Tuesday, so we're running a special on all V-necks, tank tops, and even hoodies. What's more, you'll find everything else you'll need for a casual afternoon in my company. So gear up and meet me outside in ten."

"Branch, I—"

Her sputtered protests fell on deaf ears, and the resigned look on her face showed that, what was more, Avery knew it.

Branch nudged her hip, the simple touch sending shockwaves through his loins even as her look of mock protest— and surprise—thrilled him to no end. For once, the smartest girl he knew was speechless, and Branch couldn't have been prouder to have been the one to render her so.

"My company," he interrupted her weak protests with the same bossy baritone with which he corralled the rowdy *kids* into their weekly brainstorming sessions. "My rules. Now gear up and meet me outside in ten, Avery."

She crossed her arms over her small but firm breasts, putting on a playful pout and meeting his eyes with a mock look of dissent. "Or what, Big Guy?"

The term of endearment was so surprising it nearly took his breath away. "Or I give your pops a quick call and tell him how poorly our first meeting went."

"Branch Asher, so help me, God, if you aren't the most insufferable SOB on the planet!"

He ignored her feigned protests and tapped the *Apple* watch on his wrist. "You. Me. Ten, out here." He hooked a thumb over his shoulder at the warehouse door before pressing through it and out into another glorious California afternoon.

Chapter Five: Avery

"I feel ridiculous . . ."

Branch clapped his hands in sheer, unmitigated joy as Avery sauntered out of the warehouse door into the dazzling blue-orange sunshine of a flawless west coast afternoon. "You look marvelous, babe. Drop-dead gorgeous." As if she didn't already feel humiliated enough, he gave her an overexaggerated chef's kiss for good measure. "Ten out of ten. Bravo!"

She'd forgotten how playful Branch could be. How temptingly teasing and intoxicatingly, utterly infuriating. And how much she'd adored him for it. Not that they'd ever spoken about it, of course. Or spoken much at all, for that matter. But from afar, watching him tear apart opponents in Speech class or go toe-to-toe with some dim-witted bully in the middle of the cafeteria, she'd always admired his rapier wit and cocky sarcasm. If only she'd been half as ballsy as Branch had been growing up, ballsy enough to introduce herself, that was, they could have actually been friends.

Or, as she'd often hoped over the years, so much more.

She glanced down at her ridiculous outfit, the best Branch's stupid gift shop had to offer, which wasn't much if you weren't a seventeen-year-old dweeb eager to wear the poster of your favorite, outdated, cheesiest horror movie on a surprisingly soft V-neck baby doll tee. It vaguely matched the off-white pajama shorts and the black and white sandals she'd chosen to replace her dramatic black heels.

"I never took you for a *Werewolf Bikers from Hell* fan, Avery."

"It was the only one in my size, moron."

He gave her a leering grin she felt all the way to her ovaries. Jesus, he hadn't changed a bit. Except, that was, for the better. She thought she'd forgotten the long-simmering crush she'd had on Lakemont High's resident aloof, bespectacled, bookish nerd, but it had only been dormant, hibernating until this very moment to come out from under some rock and drag her back to teenage lust and make her act like some dewy schoolgirl all over again. "I'd . . . hardly call that your size, Avery. I mean, if you breathe too hard, it might tear right the hell off."

"So maybe you should invest in an inventory control company to round out your umbrella of diversified holdings, Big Shot. That way, you can keep your stupid gift shop stocked with clothes for, you know, actual women."

He nodded and tapped the *notes* feature on his phone. "Good idea," he murmured, before making a digital note to do just that. "I've been meaning to invest in something like that. See, I've already bought into one of your pitches, Avery. When you report back to Daddy tonight, you can tell him all about it."

"I'm glad you're enjoying yourself, Branch," she said, approaching the bike rack where he stood, rakishly handsome as his long, expressive fingers clung to the handlebars of two matching beach cruisers.

"Oh, I am. And once you hop on one of these puppies, you're going to be as well."

Avery paused midway to the gleaming metal rack. "Branch, it's been years since I rode one of those things. Manhattan isn't exactly pedal-friendly, okay?"

"Avery, it's literally like riding a bike. Scratch that. It *is* riding a bike. You pedal around and go forward, and you keep doing that until you get where you're going, and you jump off, and that's that. And if you forget for just a second, don't worry, there's grass on either side of the bike path so you can just fall onto that."

"How reassuring."

Of course he was right. She relaxed her vice-like grip on the pebbly rubber handlebars as the pedals wound smoothly round and round, her bare legs flexing in fresh air for once and not the sleek exercycles in the corporate gym.

"See?" Branch gloated as he steered them gently away from the warehouse and gradually north, down a wide swath of sidewalk that looked freshly paved and very user-friendly. "Told you it would come back to you."

"It better have, as much as I rode one of these back in school."

"You had to. Once you refused to go away to boarding school, your dad revoked your allowance, remember?"

"How . . . how did you know that?"

He slightly blushed. Or perhaps it was just the effort of pedaling away from his surprisingly low-key and anonymous corporate offices that had his cheeks so flushed. "I heard you talking to your crew about it one day."

"Yeah, I guess I had a pretty big mouth back then."

"And a pretty big chip on your shoulder, as I recall. At least, when it came to your old man, that is."

Avery gave a noncommittal shrug. It felt surreal to be back in Lakemont again, period. And even more so to be cruising down its streets with Branch Asher. And to hear him psychoanalyzing her turbulent teenage years to boot? The moment was downright Twilight Zone-esque.

"That's how it is with stepfathers, you know?"

He smirked, gently swerving in her general direction and making her wobble uncertainly. He chuckled quietly to himself and swerved back into his own lane. "Billionaire stepfathers who couldn't understand why you didn't join him in Manhattan, no doubt."

"Yes," she murmured, struggling to ignore the triggers that

being back in her old hometown provided, free of charge in her head. "Especially after the divorce."

Branch nodded, as if aware their sunny roadside field trip had taken a stiff detour straight to Trigger Town.

Before he could dredge up any more of her sordid past, she sighed, hitting her stride as they rode side by side down the gently curving sidewalk that led away from the drab exterior of his corporate headquarters and toward a new development slightly more vibrant and energetic. "Where are we going, anyway?"

He seemed to brighten as well. "You remember old Carver's Mill?"

She brightened, back on familiar territory. "I thought this road looked familiar. But . . . where's the mill?"

"Only in our memories, Avery. I had it torn down to create Vintage Village."

"Vintage Village?"

He gave her a disapproving nod so reminiscent of her stepfather's that she had to do a double take to make sure the old man hadn't joined them on their mid-afternoon bike ride. "Have you done no research on me before you flew in to present your pitch? I mean, sheesh . . ."

She vaguely recalled the name from one of his numerous corporate holdings, but there were so many that she'd lost track and had promptly given up memorizing them all on the *Learjet* over. Between the snack bars and game rooms and roller rinks and diners and cafes, all themed around a particular era in time, to say nothing of the popular media of that time — records, music, books, stars, movies, etc. — Branch had created an actual empire all his own.

No wonder Branch didn't think he needed her help.

As they distanced themselves from the wide, sprawling warehouse at the heart of Branch's HQ, they wound toward the unmistakable hum of a small but thriving entertainment center on the far side of town.

Sure enough, the signs they passed for it read, *Welcome to Vintage Village, next four entrances.* Neon, and plenty of it, glowed in the dimming California sun as Branch gently steered them toward one of the four parking lots. To his credit, Branch let her digest each new establishment as they passed, slowly, putting the *cruise* in the beach cruisers they pedaled gently through the rollicking entertainment district.

She noted, in no particular order, Spare Change, a thriving arcade featuring posters of retro games like *Ms. Pac-Man* and *Galaga* in the windows, a video rental store called, aptly enough, *Rewind,* a larger souvenir stand like the one she'd chosen her current wardrobe from called *Timeless Threads* and even a retro diner called *Neon Nights* decked out in 80s-themed pink and blue neon, like something out of an episode of *Miami Vice.*

Though it was still only mid-afternoon, the parking lots were mostly full, and folks of all ages milled about the care-fully themed and equally curated Vintage Village.

"This . . . is all you?"

"Not to brag," he bragged, "but . . . duh."

They continued to skirt the parking lots, one by one, cruis-ing slowly through Branch's own little thriving empire. "When the hell did you do all this?"

Chapter Six: Branch

"While you were off getting your MBA, hot pants."

Branch admired the width of Avery's deep green eyes, always so expressive they could never hide a thing, even when she was supposed to be negotiating the deal of a lifetime.

She turned to him, face gently shadowed by the spiffy new ballcap she'd chosen in the warehouse gift shop. The baby doll t-shirt, sandals, and hat made her look all of eighteen again. And in all the right ways. "I mean, I knew the *Creature Café* was popular, but . . . all this? From . . . just that?"

"Like I said, Avery. While you were away getting a degree or two to hang on your wall, I was still here, hitting the bricks and pounding the pavement and getting a Ph.D. in the School of Hard Knocks. Along the way, I came up with a few good ideas that folks seemed to love, and every year, I make it my mission to come up with a few more. That . . . adds up, I suppose, over time."

"To all this?"

Branch swerved his bike gently toward her again, thrilled to see her flinch at his sudden appearance in her peripheral vision. "You're . . . not very good at keeping a poker face, Avery." She clearly wasn't even trying anymore.

"Forgive me if I'm a tad surprised by all this. It's one thing to read a spreadsheet and quite another to see the investments come to life right before my very own eyes."

"That's the best part, Avery. That's why my HQ is a warehouse and not some drab office building in some research park. No doors, no corner suites, just people, passion, ideas, and developments, all day long. That's why I want you to stick around and see what Asher Enterprises is all about before you make some generic offer the bean counters back home cooked up to valuate my company, sight unseen."

"Funny." She smirked, weaving her bike back toward him in a surprisingly deft manner and meeting his gaze in a most challenging, even flirtatious, way. "And here I thought it was just to get in my pants."

CHAPTER SEVEN: AVERY

"Speaking of," Branch murmured, unable to hide the blush that had suddenly crept up to flatter his still adorable dimples. "Where are you staying while you're in town?"

Avery struggled to keep her expression neutral, a smile fixed on her suddenly thin lips. She hadn't meant to blurt out something so provocative after what seemed like only a few minutes in town, but something about Branch sent her inhibitions flying straight out the window.

None of this seemed real, somehow. The promotion, the boardroom, the flight, the arrival back in her hometown after so long spent away from it, the sudden appearance of Branch in his own office, long and limber and looking as if he'd just stepped out of their high school yearbook, fresh and willing and supple right before her very own eyes.

Was it her fault she couldn't help herself? Was it her fault the whole moment felt like playing hooky? Was it her fault she was drunk off the sight of him, sounding like some idiot fangirl?

She struggled to regain what was left of her former composure. "The old house, obviously."

He nodded as if surprised. "Obviously."

"I mean, it's still here, it's still empty, it's still close, so . . . why not?"

He gave her a snide little smirk. "I tried to buy it a few years back."

She gave him a scolding glance, suddenly defensive. "You shouldn't have, Branch."

He seemed surprised she'd react in such a manner. Business was business, clearly. "Why not? It's in a great little district I'm trying to convert to a strip mall."

She rolled her eyes, warming to the bike ride, the beautiful California weather, and even the forced *vacation* away from her new duties at Balthazar Broadcasting. Maybe, she reasoned, a little time away, a little distance, wouldn't be so bad after all.

Warming to the new parameters of her assignment, Avery adopted a suddenly sassy tone. "Aww, just what Lakemont needs . . . another strip mall."

"Anyway . . ." He waved a hand as they exited Vintage Village, bound for parts unknown. She hadn't expected to be riding a bike in the sultry California sunshine when she'd woken up in gritty New York City that morning, let alone wearing a skimpy set of souvenir clothes next to her high school crush. Thus, it seemed wherever they went, for as long as it took, was a welcome surprise that only added to the surreal nature of her impromptu homecoming. "It wasn't going to be just another strip mall, Avery."

"Naturally," she murmured, admiring the shimmering neon and sheer audacity of what Branch had created from what was literally an abandoned sawmill on the edge of a sleepy little town. "But you really shouldn't have."

"Why not?"

Avery idly wondered if Branch really realized the power her father wielded or, for that matter, his stubbornness when going after something he truly wanted. "It's probably what alerted Dad to your presence in the first place, Branch."

"You think?"

"I mean, we may not have a cool, funky warehouse full of actual infants at *our* corporate headquarters, but we do have a division just for monitoring sketchy property acquisitions in towns where we have a vested interest, sure."

"Sketchy? Hardly."

She gave him a good study, surprised to find them cruising past the warehouse again and back toward the heart of small, folksy Lakemont, California. "No, probably not, but no doubt it set off a red flag back at Balthazar HQ when someone tried to buy the old homestead."

He made a face. "Not sure why your father would want to hold onto it in the first place."

"Me, either, frankly. It was Mom's childhood home, after all. They rarely used it while they were married. Mom said it was because it reminded him that she came from the wrong side of the tracks."

"So why'd he marry her then?"

"She was a stewardess. They met in first-class. I guess he saw something in her he liked. Hired her away from the airline to work on his *Learjet*, and well, the rest was history."

He gave her a knowing wink. "I'll never forget that first day you showed up for school after your parents broke up midway through freshman year."

She rolled her eyes as they cruised through the small, rustic town her mother had called home. "God, I was definitely going through my rebellious phase back then."

"I'll say. You spent more time in detention than you did in a real class."

"Yeah, well, I had Dad threatening to disown me in one ear and Mom running him down every day after school in the other. It's a miracle I graduated in the first place."

Branch's voice was low, and, dare she say, wistful. "I wish . . . you hadn't."

Avery gave him a curious glance. "Why not?"

"Then you might not have left the way you did."

She nodded, flattered he would even notice. He'd barely even spoken to her back in school. Suddenly he was giving her a guided tour of his own private lakeside empire?

Branch's cryptic, curious demeanor was only adding to the surreal nature of her first trip back home since then. After her mother passed from a brief but staggering illness just before Avery graduated high school, there'd been no reason to stick around Lakemont.

Other than Branch, that was.

College awaited, and with it, at long last, her stepfather's begrudging approval as she began taking her first business classes on the way to her eventual MBA. She threw herself into her studies. It was partly a way to work through the grief of losing her mother and partly to prove to her stepfather that she belonged, once and for all, on the right side of the tracks.

As if in a flash, six years and multiple degrees had flown by until here she was, a block away from the house she'd grown up in and next to the boy who had, once again, given her new life.

Chapter Eight: Branch

"Hey, where are you going?" Branch called out to Avery as she cruised straight past the house at 249 Lakemont Avenue.

She screeched to a stop and did a lazy circle in the empty cul-de-sac before joining him on the curb in front of the newly renovated house.

Her face was as surprised as he was delighted. "I . . . what have they done to it?"

He smirked, wondering if she'd notice. "They've been busy, that's for sure."

"It's . . . unrecognizable."

"That's a bad thing?"

She slugged him playfully on the shoulder. He relished the touch. "I mean, sure, it was always a tad on the scruffy side back in the day, but . . . after Mom's health started declining, I just didn't have the heart to keep it up."

Branch nodded soberly. As always, Avery recovered quickly. She'd never let herself dwell on the past too long, even when it was still somewhat in the present. "Well, the property management company sure has. Seems like every month they're tweaking something around here. A new roof, fancy landscaping, plenty of renovations in the front and back. They've been at it for years."

"Why, though? Dad told me himself he'd never set foot in this *one-stoplight town* again, as he always called it."

"Maybe he always figured you'd come back one day?"

They walked their bikes up to the garage as Avery glanced

curiously at a glowing keypad just outside the door. She turned to him with a conspiratorial grin, making him feel like one of the in-crowd after all.

"I wonder if the old code still works?" she asked as she pressed a series of green glowing numbers. Sure enough, the new door slid up smoothly, revealing an empty and austere garage that looked as sterile and glossy as something out of a model home.

"Where did all the junk go?" Avery marveled, stepping cautiously inside as if it might be some kind of a trap.

"Probably a storage shed somewhere?"

"The dump is more like it. Dad never was the sentimental type. And God knows he had six years of me matriculating to do whatever he wanted around here."

They stood in front of a gleaming new washer and dryer set, the only things other than tile, drywall, and cement in the spacious two-car garage.

"I mean, was there anything you wanted to keep from back then?"

Several emotions crossed Avery's face before she pressed the same code on an interior panel. Grabbing the doorknob with one hand, she tapped her forehead with the other. "Everything I wanted from this house, I have up here, Branch."

He nodded and she stepped inside, both of them admiring the hardwood floors and sleek, modern furnishings of what might as well have been a vacation rental. It even smelled like a hotel room.

"The hell?" Avery marveled as she ran her hands along a leather sofa with an unmistakably low flat Scandinavian design.

Branch nodded, wishing he had the kind of style and flair the property manager's interior designer clearly did. He made a mental note to ask her at some point. After all, as funky and fresh as it already was, the warehouse could always use a fancy new makeover.

"Maybe he's staging it for sale after all?" he offered, admiring a spiffy ladder bookshelf lined with artsy, if generic, doodads and knickknacks.

They shared a glance, standing in the middle of the spacious, softly lit living room much closer than they had back in his office. High windows, and many of them, gave the room a natural light that made the minimalist décor all the more enticing. Beyond the living room's sliding glass doors, a similarly sleek patio set beckoned, and beyond that, a shimmering pool that was just as clearly well-maintained.

"Bizarre," Avery murmured, fingering the fringes of a vaguely Bohemian wall-hanging featuring a macrame rainbow next to an antique gold mirror.

"Someone knew you were coming," Branch announced, pointing to a single piece of silver stationery resting atop a jar candle on the kitchen counter.

CHAPTER NINE: AVERY

"The hell?"

Avery reached for the envelope, embossed with her father's initials in glossy, shimmering silver. He'd been using the same stationery since she'd gone to college, and the envelope itself was an immediate trigger. How many reprimands she'd gotten throughout her six years at *Brown* on similar notecards.

She opened it carefully, Branch hovering nearby as if he couldn't wait to see who it was from. "Do you mind?" she playfully teased as he stood his ground. It was hard to concentrate with his lithe, limber body standing so close, to say nothing of his musky cologne and radiating body heat.

If Avery had thought that tooling around town would wear off some of the sexy sheen of being next to Branch Asher, she'd been sorely mistaken. If anything, his ruddy tan skin and effortless beauty was making her as hot under the collar as the impromptu cardio session through town.

"Come on, I've come this far." He nudged her shoulder, sending her senses into overdrive.

"Why are you here, anyway?" She chuckled, waving the notecard unread in one hand as she not-so-insistently pushed him away with the other.

He remained steadfast, hovering pleasantly right behind her as if . . . waiting for something. For what, she had no idea, though her mind's eye flashed on a dozen different fantasies from back in school she wouldn't mind making come true while she was forced to stay in town. She brushed away the ridiculous thought, struggling to focus on what he was currently saying instead of admiring his thick, full lips and how they might taste against her own.

"Like I said, I plan on buying this place one day, Avery. I just wanted to see what I was getting."

She clucked a tongue and pointed the envelope menacingly in his face. "Blue in the face is what you're going to get if you plan on holding your breath before this house is up for sale. I'll outbid you any day of the week."

"With what, Avery? Your daddy's allowance?"

"Branch Asher, so help me God—"

"Just read it already," he teased, still knowing how to get her goat.

"Fine," she murmured, glancing at the first line on the card that read "Welcome home." And below it, "Good luck with the merger." There was a PS at the bottom of the note, in her father's scrawling script, surprisingly thoughtful for a man who'd basically thrown her to the wolves with her very first assignment. "Check the fridge, thought you might be hungry after your flight."

Before she could do just that, Branch was already gripping the nearest handle of the gleaming stainless-steel fridge, clearly making himself at home and in no danger of leaving anytime soon.

If she knew what was good for her, Avery should have kicked him out the minute he tried to slide his foot across the welcome mat just outside her door. And barring that, she should have never let him past the small but tidy kitchenette, to say nothing of the living room just beyond.

So why was she squirming where she stood, struggling to control her wicked thoughts and feeling the long-buried ember of desire beginning to smolder yet again deep in her loins? Why was she mentally undressing him and wondering if he was a boxers or briefs man? And how long would it take her to drag either of them down around his long, skinny ankles?

With her teeth, naturally.

"Do you mind, Branch?" She struggled to pretend as if she didn't want him here, doing this very thing, acting just this way.

He winked, dramatically whisking the refrigerator door open as if modeling a new prize on *The Price is Right*. Inside was a bevy of treats more suitable for a weekend getaway than an overnight business deal — champagne and strawberries, fresh meats and cheeses, crackers and crudites as far as the eye could see.

"Damn!" Branch grabbed a bottle of champagne, already tearing at the gold foil wrapper before she could protest.

As if . . .

"I beg your pardon," she murmured, even as she studied the cherry wood cabinets until she found two crystal flutes among a smattering of glassware for two. She was surprised to find her hands subtly trembling as they gripped the long, stemmed flute glasses.

He pretended to act all innocent, despite the leering glance at her across the kitchen counter. "What? You must be parched after your trip."

She lingered nearby, too close for her own good as she teased him playfully. "I mean, maybe if you'd offered me a bottle of water at your fancy warehouse, Branch, or a meal at one of your many restaurant chains as we pedaled past, I might not be."

"Well, I'm making up for it now, aren't I?" He popped the cork, sending it flying into a potted snake plant halfway across the room.

"Yeah, punk, with *my* champagne."

He topped off their flutes expertly, long fingers gripping the bottle as he gently drifted back from glass to glass until they were nearly full to the brim. He handed her one, grabbing the other and pausing momentarily before taking a sip.

"What shall we toast to, Avery?" He was mock-serious, bordering on flirty. She found the combination, to say nothing of the man, hard to resist.

If not impossible.

Was this what it felt like, she wondered idly, *to finally lose your damn mind and fall head over heels on the first date?* If so, Avery decided that she didn't mind it one little bit.

"You, accepting my offer," she teased, although the odds of that seemed further and further off with every new development in their ongoing saga. Branch was clearly a self-made man and was doing just fine without the help of her billionaire father, thanks very much.

Then again, she realized, standing in a too-small t-shirt and ill-fitting cotton drawstring shorts that threatened to come loose and slide down her legs at any moment, she wasn't exactly acting very professional on her end, either.

If she had been, Avery realized, she would have ended the meeting back in the warehouse. Every moment since then, she knew, was just begging for trouble.

Good trouble, she realized, wondering just how good Branch could be and whether or not she'd be given a chance to find out.

He frowned, shaking his head. "How about . . . to a successful partnership."

"Yeah, right," she murmured, clinking his glass all the same.

"Seriously," he said, the glass still hovering in midair as if he refused to drink it until she saw the wisdom of his toast. "I think we'd make a great team."

"Funny," she said with a smirk before taking a sip of the dry, crisp bubbly. "I thought you had to be a literal teenager to work for Asher Enterprises."

"I mean, it helps, but I'll overlook the slight age discrepancy in this case."

"You do know we're both twenty-five, right?"

"And look at us, Avery. You're the head of your own division at one of the biggest broadcasting companies in literally the world, and I'm, well . . . look how far we've come."

She took another sip before setting the glass down on the marble countertop, leaning next to it as she drank in his long, limber body and youthful features. Despite his age, he still looked like the secretly sexy nerd she'd fallen in lust with six years ago. "I always knew you'd go far, Branch."

"Bullshit." He scoffed, topping off their glasses without being asked. He leaned against the opposite counter in the small but tidy kitchenette to give her a good study. The way his eyes drank her in, from top to bottom and back again, made her shiver in all the right places, and wet in all the wrong ones. "Admit it, Avery, you thought I was a nerd who'd end up working in a comic book store or something someday."

She snorted. "Okay, sure, but now you own the comic book store. Or, at least, the comic book store slash coffee shop known as *Comix Café*."

He chuckled, finally impressed. "So you *have* been reading up on me."

She tapped the folder sticking out of her valise. "I told you already, Branch. Failure is not an option here."

"And I told *you*, Avery, you're going to have to adjust your definition of failure because under no circumstances am I being bought out by your billionaire father just so he can franchise all my hard work and treat my young, creative, brilliant, sweet, funny, hardworking and mostly loyal employees like, forgive my French, shit."

"Whoa, whoa, pardner," she cautioned, raising her hands in defense. "Who said anything about franchising?"

"Why else would he send you here, Avery?"

She struggled to rein his sudden outburst back in. "You'll find out, Branch, when you hear my pitch."

"And I'll hear your pitch when I'm good and ready." He huffed, quaffing his champagne quickly as if to soothe his frazzled nerves. "As in, three short days from now."

She rolled her eyes and reached for the champagne bottle. He was right. After all, she *was* parched. "God, were you always this infuriating?"

"You might have known," Branch assured her, holding out his glass for a much-needed refill. "If you'd ever bothered to talk to me back in school."

"How could I?" she shot back, waving her glass for effect. "Hiding the way you did behind those thick glasses and that even thicker stack of books you always carried around with you everywhere."

"You're one to talk, Avery. I might have hid behind a stack of books, but you always had your entourage of mean girls and jock buddies to hide behind. Good luck trying to penetrate that particular clique."

She chuckled, surprised at how quickly the bubbly had gone to her head. He noticed, jutting out his chin at her defensively. "You think that's funny?"

"You said penetrate," she explained, sounding all of thirteen.

He started to protest, then chuckled himself. "Wow, you . . . who are you, anyway? Who is this suddenly spontaneous, funny, sarcastic, wacky new chick dressed up as Avery Balthazar?"

She glanced down at the bubbles fizzing atop her crystal champagne flute, more wistful than she thought she'd be, given the humorously insane circumstances.

"I wish I knew, Branch," she murmured thoughtfully, as surprised by the question as she was by the juvenile behavior that had prompted it.

Penetrate? Really? What the hell was she thinking? Still, it had come out, and now that it had, there was no putting the genie back in the bottle. She sighed and glanced his way, surprised at how comfortable she was talking to him all of a sudden. After all, they'd said more in the last half-hour than they'd said in four years of high school. All the same, be it the jet lag, the homecoming, or simply half a bottle of bubbly on an empty stomach, Avery was suddenly in a confessional mood.

And who better to confess to than her boyhood crush?

"You know, Branch, I was dreading this trip at first, but now that I'm finally here, maybe . . . maybe I can find out who I really am, you know? What's really important to me?"

He set down his champagne flute, pinning her with a soft brown gaze that seemed to see into her very soul. "You know, don't take this the wrong way, Avery, but when you walked into my office earlier today, in that pantsuit, all gussied up, slinging that valise like some kind of bulletproof vest, it kind of looked like you were playing dress up."

She snorted, tugging at the hem of her baby doll tee as if to cover the butterflies currently dancing around in her nervous belly. She felt, under his gaze, positively and utterly naked. Bare before his eyes and vulnerable to his every whim and whimsy. She only wished she didn't like the feeling so damn much.

"And this doesn't?" She huffed, sounding all of seven years old.

He pushed himself gently away from the countertop. She braced herself, not sure for what. Her fight or flight reaction was in high gear, making her pulse pound and her heart race even as she froze in place, waiting for Branch to make the next move.

Whatever that might be . . .

His voice was low, buttery, and smooth, and Avery

suddenly realized, trustworthy. She hung on every word as he murmured, sweetly, "Honestly, Avery? You look just like the girl I've been crushing on for the last six years."

She rolled her eyes, only hoping that much could be true. "You're just saying that to get out of hearing my pitch, Branch Asher."

His eyes were pure and right and true, penetrating hers in a sincere way that thrilled her to the core. He might have been acting like a downright cocky bastard ever since she'd gotten into town, but Branch was no actor — that much was clear. She struggled to believe him, even as his passion poured through in every syllable.

"I'm saying it, Avery, because I've been wanting to say it ever since we graduated. Was trying to say it the night we graduated, before your dad whisked out of town in his private jet and stole you away in that big, fancy limousine before the ceremony was even over."

Branch was close, too close, forcing her to look slightly up at the warm embers in his soft brown eyes. She wanted to back away, to run and start everything over, to not be here at all. At the same time, she couldn't imagine being anywhere else at that very moment, nor with anyone else on the planet.

"You could have told me before that night," she croaked.

His hand reached out, tentatively. She thought he might clasp her chin and turn her face up for a kiss. She wondered, idly, what she might do if that were the case. Instead, he slid a stray lock of black hair behind her ear. Suddenly, Avery wasn't sure which gesture was sexier.

"I don't think I could have said it then, Avery. Honestly? I can . . . I can hardly say it now."

Chapter Ten: Branch

"So why are you then?"

Her voice was just above a whisper. Or, perhaps, it was the sound of Branch's own heart pounding that drowned out her garbled reply. "Because I never thought I'd see you again," he confessed, hardly believing he was spilling his guts this way, this soon, least of all to the woman that broke his heart. Whether she ever knew it or not. "And I promised myself that night we graduated, as you drove off in that big ass limousine, that if I ever saw you again, if you ever came back home and actually gave me the time of day, that I wouldn't waste the chance to . . . to tell you how I feel."

"We were kids, Branch," she murmured, peering up into his eyes and not backing away from his advance.

"We're still kids, Avery. At least, I feel like a kid when I'm around you."

She set her champagne glass down, glancing gently away. "Is that all you were gonna say that night, Branch? That night on the football field before my father's limousine pulled up, and I ran away, still wearing my graduation gown."

"Ran away? I thought . . . he forced you to go."

She shook her head almost imperceptibly. "I could have stayed, Branch."

"Then . . . why didn't you?"

She swallowed so hard even Branch could hear it. Peered back up at him, an almost frail look of defiance gleaming in her gentle green eyes. "Because I knew if I did, I knew if I let you say what you were going to say that night, or if I said what I'd wanted to say, that . . . that I'd never want to leave Lakemont after that. And if I didn't leave then, at that very moment, I knew I probably never would."

His chuckle was a dry gust of relief. "Would that have been so bad, Avery?"

She glanced away again. Reached for her glass, then seemed to think better of it. Looked back up at him and nodded his way. "Answer my question first."

"Which one?" He was confused. Befuddled was more like it. Suddenly, he couldn't think straight, let alone remember what she'd asked him five seconds ago.

"What else were you going to say that night, Branch?" Her tone was vaguely pleading, slightly teasing, and suddenly, inescapably flirtatious.

His heart pounded. Blood rushed through his ears. His hands trembled as he gripped the countertop on either side of her, as if to steady himself. Or, perhaps, trap her in place for what was about to come next.

"I wasn't going to *say* anything, Avery," he confessed.

She seemed surprised. Genuinely sincerely surprised. "No? What then?"

He paused for only a moment, as if to give himself one last chance to escape. Or, maybe, to give Avery one last chance to flee. Then he quickly, gently, almost chastely brushed her lips with his own.

She gasped.

He wasn't mistaking it this time. Gasped and flinched, but he noticed she didn't pull back. Didn't grunt or run or push him away or, for that matter, protest at all. The gentle kiss barely hinted at more, at so much more, but even as she leaned gently into it, he pulled back, as if gun shy to start something neither of them could possibly finish.

"That," he murmured, stepping back slightly and watching her eyelids flutter and her lips droop as she sank back against the countertop behind her. "That's what I was going to do that night."

She stared at her sandals, face aglow with a wicked crimson blush, heart pounding in her chest. "Oh."

"Oh? That's all you can say?" He wasn't mad, exactly. Or even hurt, particularly. Just suddenly . . . curious.

She glanced up, looking both apologetic and abjectly confused. "I . . . it's kind of hard to talk right now."

He chuckled, knowing the feeling all too well. "Well, at least try. I mean, hell, I just poured out my heart to you, girl!"

She chuckled nervously, glancing back up at him, the blush unavoidable in her usually pale, hollow cheeks. "I guess, I mean . . . you should have. You should have kissed me that night. You should have grabbed my arm and turned me around and told me all that and then kissed me."

"What for? It wouldn't have changed your mind."

"It might have, Branch. And then . . ."

"Then what?"

"Then we might have seen what it would have felt like to be partners, like you said."

His heart kickstarted into overdrive again. He could hardly believe what he was hearing. He searched her eyes for confirmation. "Would you . . . like that, Avery?"

"I might, Branch. I mean . . . I'm willing to try, for these next few days at least, to see . . . to see how that might feel. Uh, partnering with you, I mean."

He took another step closer, watching her flinch at the motion. Then she softened, a sly smile curling to her ripe, full lips. Jesus, Branch could hardly believe he'd just kissed those very same lips.

Suddenly, now, after all those years of regretting he'd never kissed them when he'd had the chance. Then again, who was he fooling? He was all bluster and bravado now, but back then? He'd never had a chance. Or if he'd had the chance, he'd certainly never had the guts. But that was then, and this was now.

Now? He had guts aplenty. And no one to share them with. Then again, Avery seemed suddenly willing to rewrite history with him. Or was he just imagining things again?

"Be careful what you wish for," he warned her with a playfully menacing growl, continuing to test the waters as the day took another, most unexpected and scintillating turn.

"Stop talking, big boy," she practically purred, tugging him closer by his vintage snowman tie. "Or I might just renege on my offer."

Chapter Eleven: Avery

"Avery, I . . ." Branch stood in front of her, as if unsure how to proceed. He'd been all balls and bragging moments ago but suddenly stood on far more uncertain ground. "I mean . . ."

"Ugh," she blurted, tugging him even closer as she stood to her full height and willed herself to take charge of the situation before they both lost their mojo and missed another opportunity to express what were obviously stronger feelings than both of them cared to admit. "You're the one who started this, Branch! Do I have to do everything myself?"

She kissed him before he could stammer out a reply, hard and fast, as if to make sure all of this was really, actually happening. It was nothing like their first kiss, which had felt more like a question mark.

This?

This kiss was definitely an exclamation point!

Somehow, she managed to magically turn him around, tugging him by his tie until his back was to the counter instead of hers. Sunlight streamed in from the high, open windows, bathing his face in radiant light even as she loosened the knot on his tie and gently dragged it from his collar.

She let it pile onto the countertop, coiling like a red and green snake as she turned her attention to the buttons of his soft white Oxford dress shirt. "I . . . I can help," he blathered before she silenced him with another withering, sputtering kiss.

"You can help by stopping all the talking." She huffed,

admiring the glistening skin of his smooth torso beneath his shirt as she continued to unbutton it, fingers trembling as she danced ever closer to his beltline.

"Avery, we . . ."

"Stop. Talking. Branch!"

She tugged the shirt free at last, dragging it over each gleaming shoulder as she let it fall atop the tie on the marble countertop. "Just . . . sit back and let a girl indulge in her high school fantasy, okay?"

He stood, chest gleaming and smooth and surprisingly toned for a nerd. Make that a reformed nerd. He'd clearly grown up since high school, and just as clearly . . . in all the right places.

"You . . . you fantasized about this?" he sputtered, clearly disbelieving even as he stood, half-naked from her eager hands, as if she was going to elaborate lengths to punk him.

"Only every day in homeroom, nerd, so . . . stop spoiling it with all your talking. From now on, just . . . sit back and enjoy, okay?"

He grinned, almost nervously, that cocky smirk smothered vaguely by a momentary dash of unsteadiness. She liked that look. Liked keeping him on his toes, literally and figuratively. Branch started to speak, saw the look in her eyes, then quickly thought better of that particular idea. She savored the silence, the pause, the anticipation, pouring her suddenly hungry eyes over every inch of Branch's long, supple physique. He'd always been tall and gangly back in school, and that alone had been enough to drive her heart, soul, and panties wild.

Now? Forget about it.

She paused, hands on his belt, leaning gently forward to kiss his throat with hungry, eager lips. He swallowed, Adam's apple dancing across her feverish lips as he murmured and gently shifted beneath her adoring kisses.

His skin tasted like sweat and fresh cut grass and warm,

smooth, masculine musk. She savored every inch of him, kissing and pecking at his taut, rouged nipples as he squirmed and murmured approval with every dance of her flickering, tempting tongue. There had been a moment there, the slightest hesitation, where she considered putting a halt to the madness, stopping the insanity, and simply kicking Branch out before taking a suitably cold shower to bring her back to her senses. At the first taste, hell, at first sight of his half-naked chest, all that—all everything—flew right out the window. She was tumbling now, falling headfirst into his charms, and she couldn't have stopped herself if she'd tried.

Not even if he'd tried. And from the bulge just beneath her hands, the only thing Branch was trying at the moment was to break free of his pants.

Avery was no prude. She was, after all, a reformed sorority girl. Still, it had been years since she'd taken the time to indulge in anything other than her fast-paced, AP honors-level curriculum. Now, the dry spell at an imminent end, she found herself daring to do things she would never have before.

Like pinning her high school crush to the kitchen counter while nibbling on his left nipple on her first day back in town, for instance. He winced deliciously, even as he leaned into the kiss with a stiffly toned chest and a deep, guttural purr.

He tried to reach for her once, and despite how badly she wanted his hands all over her, she grunted and murmured one last command. "Hands at your sides, big boy. You'll get your chance . . . *if* you're good!"

He frowned in delighted disappointment.

"Don't worry, Branch," she assured him, finally tackling the leather of his tailored belt. "I promise to make it worth the wait."

Branch merely nodded, eyes half-lidded, lips gently parted, as the sounds of his unbuckling made her panties wet with sheer, almost uncontrollable anticipation. She could see his bulge beneath his khaki linen pants, barely hiding the girth of his hearty erection.

With the belt freed and the top button quickly undone, she unzipped him slowly, enjoying the way Branch quivered and panted with the same sense of restrained abandon she felt as the room grew small and all she could see, all she could feel, all she could hear, all she could taste, touch and experience, was Branch Asher.

His pants drizzled, slowly, down his epically long legs until they puddled at his feet. He went to step out of them, and she stopped him once more with a warning glance.

"Nuh-uh." She heaved, chest gasping as she dragged her fingertips teasingly along the waistband of his soft gray boxer briefs. "You stand right where you are, hot pants. I've got you right where I want you. Besides," she teased, sinking gently to her knees in front of him. "You don't want me to get bruises now, do you?"

Branch merely shook his head as, achingly, Avery ran her hand up and down the outline of his long, straining staff. She wasn't the only one damp with excitement, the tip of his cock, fat and round, leaking through the soft cotton panel of his briefs, tempting her to lean forward and with a not-so-chaste kiss taste his excitement before making quick work of tugging the briefs down altogether.

He stood, stiff and erect, gleaming and quivering with anticipation. He gasped at the release, even before she took hold of his throbbing base to gently keep his cock in place as she began to pepper it with less and less gentle kisses.

When it was finally glistening with delight, she kissed a pearl of precum from the gleaming tip. When he gasped, she slid her lips around the throbbing head. He tasted heavenly, Avery gorging herself on his long, thin prick as she held herself in place with a hand on each of his bony hips.

He was dripping by the time she released him, stroking

him with one hand even as she kissed his sweaty happy trail while urging him to a staggering climax.

He grunted, leaning back until the spray coated his chest, Avery's hand feeling the pulse and throb as she gently clasped his veiny shaft until the fountain became a drizzle, and achingly, she stroked him dry.

Chapter Twelve: Branch

"Thank you."

Branch's eyes fluttered open, peering down at Avery as she knelt between his knees, a curious smile on her glistening lips. She still had one hand on his softening hard-on, face aglow with apparent glee.

"For what?" he croaked, throat constricted with a combination of relief and satisfaction.

"For making one of my high school fantasies come true." Her voice was hoarsely husky.

"You? Fantasized about that? I thought . . . that was just me."

"Who knows?" she murmured as he helped her to her feet. Amazingly, she was still fully dressed. "Maybe I can read your mind."

"Oh yeah." He chuckled, finally kicking free one pant leg to reach for her waist. "Then what am I wishing right now, Avery?"

She grunted, or perhaps that was just him, exhaling as he hoisted her lithe, athletic body onto the countertop in front of him. She was flush with excitement, her eyes wide with anticipation as he righted her on the counter and lingered, face mere inches from her own as his heart continued to throb so hard he could still feel it in the sway and heft of his balls.

"You're probably wishing I weighed twenty pounds less," she teased, reaching for the bottle of champagne as if it was last call at some dive bar. She took a giant swig, eyes wide with delight as she swallowed and handed it over, frat boy style.

He savored a sip of his own, but no more so than he admired her full, bruised lips, her wide eyes, or the way her raven black ponytail had finally come partially undone during her recent, uh . . . efforts.

"Wrong," he murmured, slowly reaching for the hem of her clingy baby doll t-shirt. "I'm wishing you already had your damn clothes off."

She leaned gently back, wriggling her chest in his face as he tugged at the soft black cotton until it, too, joined the growing pile at their feet.

"Wish granted." She chuckled, Branch feasting his eyes on her utterly bare breasts. "What?" she asked, noticing and attempting to cover up. "That chamise under my pantsuit jacket today didn't leave any room for a bra, so . . ."

"Do I look like I'm complaining?" he murmured, gently tugging her hands to her sides. "Now, sit still, look pretty, and let me make one of *my* high school fantasies come true."

"Branch, I . . ." He interrupted her with a kiss, intense and molten.

"No more talking," he teased, silencing her as she settled herself on the countertop, ripe and eager, a feast just waiting to be savored.

Avery's eyes spoke volumes as he dragged his fingertips slowly up either side of her ribcage, making her shiver and squirm as he teased himself — and her — with his dizzyingly slow approach toward her arching breasts. By the time he reached his final destination, she was all aquiver, gently panting as he cupped each small, pert breast in hand while her sensitive skin sent shivers through both their bodies.

Her nipples were taut and pebbled, stiff to the touch as he teased and toyed with them endlessly, the afternoon sun casting sexy shadows across her arching back and open, expressive face. He leaned slightly forward, unabashed by the fact that he was completely, utterly naked. He pinched and teased one nipple while slathering the other with his eager lips and tongue, feeling her stiffen and arch her back to press her tender breasts against his willing mouth.

Back and forth, left to right and over again, he tweaked and kissed her into a panting lather, enjoying the anticipation and longing on Avery's face as she squeezed her eyes shut as if to restrain herself from screaming out loud.

His tongue flicked and his lips savored both breasts in turn. He made quick work of dragging her baggy pajama shorts off until she sat atop the counter in the sheer black panties she'd worn under her pantsuit.

He stood back to admire them, so thin that he could see right through to the carefully tended landing strip of manicured black thatch between her legs. For some reason, this barely disguised glimpse at her quivering sex excited him more than if she'd already been bare to the touch.

He dragged his hand down her belly, stippled with little beads of fresh sweat, hearing her moan aloud with unbridled pleasure as his fingertip traced each strand of soft, black hair just inside the pricey panties.

She spread her legs eagerly, pale and soft to the touch as he turned his attention from her chest to the thick, damp bounty between her quivering thighs. Toying with the elastic waistband, he gently dragged the panties left, then right, tugging and teasing them mercilessly down as the heat and fragrance of her lust escaped and made him even hungrier to taste what he'd desired for six long, endless years.

As her panties slid down her legs to join the pile of clothes at their feet, he sank to his knees as well, dragging her closer to pepper each thigh with ravenous kisses. She flinched and murmured, alternately shrinking away from each kiss even as she slid closer to greet them, her body clearly craving the attention even as her instincts told her she shouldn't.

He ignored those and read her body language instead, dappling her waist with soft, eager kisses as he reached beneath her legs to cup one firm, ripe cheek in his palms as his efforts—and her mewling—increased in kind.

When his lips finally pressed against her fervent clit, thick and throbbing, she bit down on a gasp he could feel deep down inside her taut, quivering belly. He circled and kissed, licked, and teased her glistening bud even as she pressed and slid against his eager tongue.

Avery tasted hot and fragrant, like he'd always imagined she would, her greed for release getting the best of her as she writhed and panted, ass clenching beneath his taut grip as, at last, she bucked and squealed high enough to break the half-dozen glass windows just overhead.

He waited her out, body trembling as if from hyperthermia even as he watched a single bead of delicious sweat drift between her pert breasts and down the clenched tautness of her pale belly. One hand drifted absently to rifle through his own sweaty brown curls as she began to thank him.

He silenced her with one firm kiss against her pulsating clit until she gripped his hair tightly and climaxed once more. He smiled, lips slathered in lust even as he waited her out, riding her waves, crests, peaks, valleys, shudders, and moans until, minutes later, spent and taut like an electric wire, she clamped damp thighs on either side of his face to hold him in place— and just out of reach.

"Please, Branch," she croaked, voice sounding as hoarse as his felt. "No more."

He squeezed each ass cheek in kind, gently sliding his hands away even as her thighs gradually released him. He sank down onto his haunches, feasting his eyes on her glistening form, freezing every inch of her achingly beautiful body in his memory as his teenage fantasy finally came to life.

She righted herself, wriggling and wincing as the last of her tremors left her just enough energy to slither from the countertop and join him, arms and legs entwined on the tiled kitchen floor.

"Jesus," she murmured as he reached for the champagne bottle and chased the taste of her creamy desire with the effortless sizzle of crisp, dry bubbly.

"You can say that again, hotpants," he murmured appreciatively as he handed her the bottle. She drank of it eagerly, both of them passing it back and forth again until it was as drained and empty as their trembling loins.

Silence filled the kitchen, then the very house, as they rested there on the kitchen floor, unabashed in their steamy nakedness. She peered at him, eyes as naked as her flushed skin, as if searching for something to say.

He winked and murmured, "Welcome back, Avery."

She chuckled, rolling her eyes and curling into him as if they'd both just found the missing piece of their own particular, lonely puzzle.

Chapter Thirteen: Avery

"Is this place yours, too?" Branch chuckled with a hint of self-deprecation and set down the wicker-wrapped bottle of house Chianti after filling both their wine glasses. "You think I'd put old *Papa Pepperoni's* out of business?"

"It *is* a landmark," Avery muttered, dreamy and content as she cast her eyes around the small, intimate Italian restaurant that had been in their neighborhood for as long as she could remember.

He sat back in his chair, dressed as he'd been earlier that day in his preppy cotton button-down and linen khaki shorts, both having seen better days after spending most of that afternoon puddled on her kitchen floor back home.

"You and your friends sure enjoyed it back in the day," he remarked, eyeing her curiously.

"I mean, sure, it was our hangout for a hot minute . . ." It had been so long since Avery had enjoyed the carefree days of high school and free afternoons and endless carbs that she'd almost forgotten.

His voice was as melancholy as the soft look in his doleful brown eyes. "I used to ride by after school and see you and the gang in here, sharing a pizza and laughing, and wondered what it might feel like to be part of that circle."

She shrugged. "It was a loose circle, Branch. People came and went depending on who was beefing with who and who was sleeping with who's boyfriend or brother or girlfriend, and trust me, it seemed like a lot more fun than it was."

He cocked his head gently, curiously. "How so?"

"Girls are catty, Branch. You know that. High school girls, in particular. There was always a little too much drama for me, and eventually, I quit coming here altogether. Then Mom got sick, and, well . . ."

Branch nodded as her voice drifted off, nibbling absently on one of the crispy breadsticks poking out of an old can of tomato sauce in the middle of the table. "Memories have a way of bending time, I guess. To me, anyway, it seemed like you were a fixture here for all of senior year."

"Sure, I mean . . . I probably only hung out here a few times, and now you've got it like some weekly thing."

He shrugged, looking effortlessly radiant in the flickering flame of a pillar candle sticking out of a similar bottle of wine next to the breadsticks. It added to the old-timey charm of the local pizzeria.

He'd skipped the tie as they'd gotten ready, the open shirt collar and his effortlessly breezy charm making it feel like they were on a first date. That was, the kind of *first date* you have after already deflowering each other in a sweaty, sticky kitchen sex frenzy in the middle of the day.

Afternoon delight, indeed!

She blushed at the thought.

He noticed. He nodded, waving a crispy baked treat at her across the red and white checkered tablecloth with a merry flourish. "Breadstick for your thoughts?"

"You don't want to know," she murmured so low she half-hoped he wouldn't hear her. Of course, he did.

"Sure I do. I asked, didn't I?"

She took the breadstick from him, waving it in the air at the half-empty pizza joint around the corner and up the block from her childhood home. "I just . . . can't believe all this is happening right now."

His eyes, so brown and gentle, were curious, not judge-y. "All what?"

"I mean, this morning, I was in the boardroom at Balthazar Broadcasting getting met with frozen stares, and tonight, here I'm breaking bread with . . . you."

"Why frozen stares?"

"You know how guys are, Branch. I'm a woman, the head of some new division nobody over the age of twenty understands, plus I'm the boss' daughter, make that, the boss' *stepdaughter*, fresh out of grad school, the new kid on the block, take your pick. I've got about seven strikes against me, and the sharks in that boardroom barely tolerate one misstep before spending the rest of their days trying to drum you out of the building."

He nodded, glancing gently away as if gathering his thoughts. "Do you like it there?"

"Like it?" She'd never really thought of it that way before. She'd been predestined to work for her stepfather since before time immemorial, it seemed. Liking it wasn't really in the cards. "I mean, do you like it here?"

He smiled. Quickly. Instantly. Sincerely, a reaction so sudden and organic she didn't doubt it for a second. "Sure, yes, absolutely. I mean, it's not LA, and it's certainly not Manhattan, but . . . it suits me and what I've set out to do with my life. I do what I love every day, with young, excited people who inspire me, and I can't wait to go to work every morning and feel that way all over again."

Her emotions felt as naked as her body had been only minutes earlier. "Wow, that . . . I'm happy for you, Branch. I . . . I can see why you're so resistant to hear my pitch."

His face tightened somewhat. Avery instantly regretted mixing business with the obvious pleasure he'd felt talking about his success. "If I thought for one moment it was *your* pitch, Avery, I'd be all ears. You know that, right? But your father's been after me since day one to get Archer Enterprises folded into his umbrella of random, meaningless businesses that vaguely have to do with movies and music and TV, and I can't tell you how dead set against that I am."

She felt only the slightest tinge of defensiveness for the empire her father had built, but she spoke her mind just the same. "They're not just random and meaningless, Branch. Every division exists to feed the next. As big as our company is, it exists for the sole purpose of entertaining people, much the same way your restaurants and cafes and snack bars and roller rinks and game rooms do."

She hadn't meant to sit up in her chair. Or talk so loud. Or wave her half-eaten breadstick menacingly until it was reduced to crumbs littering the tabletop between them.

He smiled. "I'm happy for you, Avery. I really am. But you guys don't need me to get any bigger. And I certainly don't need your father interfering with what I've managed to do here in Lakemont."

Avery should have been frustrated, ticked off, pissed, even. Instead, she leaned back in her chair, reached for her wineglass, and smirked. "Were you always this stubborn back in school?"

He gave her a wink, reaching for his wineglass as well. "You'd have known if you weren't too cool to talk to me, Avery."

Chapter Fourteen: Branch

"I'm talking to you now, aren't I?"

Branch chuckled, sipping the rich, red wine and feasting his gaze on Avery's smooth, buttery skin wherever it poked out above the simple black sundress she'd worn to dinner. It flattered her lithe, athletic body and feminine curves in a most distracting way.

In addition to stocking Avery's fridge unannounced, her father—or, more likely, her father's very capable and detail-oriented personal assistant—had arranged for her to find a brand-new wardrobe hanging in her recently refurbished bedroom closet.

"Yeah," he pointed out, setting his wineglass back down on the cheesy checkerboard tablecloth. "You're talking to me because I'm an asset you want to acquire."

She rolled her eyes and glanced at the half-empty dining room. His eyes followed hers until they both met again above the cluttered table in the pleasantly outdated neighborhood pizza parlor. "Don't flatter yourself, Branch. There are plenty of other fish in the sea, thank you very much."

He winked, hearing the bluff in her voice from a mile away. Ivy League MBA or not, Avery simply wasn't a very good liar. "Are we still talking about business here, Avery? Or . . . pleasure?"

She sighed and glanced away at an elderly couple leaving the restaurant, an analog bell ringing over the front door as they exited. "Well, you've made it clear we can't talk about business for three long, boring, stupid days, so . . . I guess it'll have to be pleasure." She huffed like a petulant teenager, slumped her shoulders, and crossed her arms, pouty face and all.

And still, she looked positively ravishing.

"We don't need to talk to . . . pleasure . . . each other," he murmured just loud enough for her to hear. "We've made that perfectly clear so far."

A soft, rosy blush crept steadily up her throat even as her gaze pinned him curiously from across the intimate table for two. "Clearly, Branch. I have to admit, I . . . I've never felt so . . . pleasured before."

His smirk tugged at sore, puffy lips that, he swore, still lingered under the sweet, achingly musky taste of her. "Same here, hot pants."

"Not sure where you learned how to do all that, Branch, but . . . you should teach a class or something."

His simmering guffaw was low and quiet. "I prefer private lessons, if you don't mind."

"Mind? Did I sound like I minded back there?"

He winked saucily over his half-empty glass of wine. "It was a little hard to hear with your thighs clenched against my ears—"

"Would you two care for anything else at the moment?"

Branch and Avery started, forgetting for a moment they were surrounded by other, actual humans until the elderly waiter—who'd probably been working at *Papa Pepperoni's* since its grand opening—set down their salads with moves so stealthy, he could have been a ninja in another life.

"This is perfect, thank you," Branch murmured, heart pounding and face blushing as he offered the elderly gent a throwaway line before the older gentleman shuffled quietly away, leaving him and Avery to savor their private table in the cozy corner by the glowing Christmas tree.

"It *has* been perfect, Branch."

He glanced back at Avery, surprised by the sudden gush of emotion from the original Mean Girl herself.

"Beg pardon?" he teased, even though he'd heard her perfectly.

She rolled her big green eyes. "You heard me, smartass."

"I did, Avery. I just . . . I'm having a hard time adjusting to the new you."

Her response was as factual as her earlier statements had been flirty, even saucy. "There's nothing new about me, Branch. I'm still the same old me I always was. You just never took the time to get to know me, and now that you have, you're surprised I'm not the bitch you always thought I was."

He tut-tutted, ignoring his salad. "I never thought you were a bitch, Avery. Far from it."

She waved her wineglass back at him. "Could have fooled me."

He smirked, no longer hungry. He'd been absolutely famished when he suggested they go for a late-night bite before the restaurant closed but suddenly couldn't think of anything but Avery, squirming atop the kitchen counter as his hands squeezed her ripe, writhing derriere.

She glanced at her uneaten salad, perhaps sharing the same sudden distaste for Italian food as himself. "Breadstick for your thoughts," she teased, waving one at him playfully.

One might even say saucily.

His response was sudden and straightforward, with a menacing glance to match. "You don't want to know, Avery."

"Sure I do, big boy," she teased, nibbling a fresh breadstick provocatively. "What, you're thinking of another high school fantasy you want to relive?"

He nodded, pretending to marvel at her non-existent ESP skills. "You don't exactly have to be Nostradamus to figure that one out, Avery."

"Not with that lecherous look in your eyes, Branch."

"I didn't hear you complaining earlier tonight."

She glanced at something, or someone, just over his shoulder. "No, and you're not likely to hear me complaining later tonight, either."

He went to make a witty remark when she interrupted him, glancing up at the elderly waiter who had suddenly appeared at their table bearing a variety of pasta dishes.

"Change of plans, sir. Can we . . . have those to go?"

CHAPTER FIFTEEN: AVERY

"Branch?"

Avery lingered under the hot spray of water, feeling ridiculous in her ill-fitting sundress even as her entire body squirmed with anticipation, imagining the tendrils of hot water dribbling across her skin much as she awaited Branch's fingertips, tracing the road map of her desire as he had only hours earlier.

It was hard to hear under the running water, the master bathroom having been completely redone like the rest of the house as she found herself surrounded by crystal clear glass and more stainless-steel fixtures while her bare feet wriggled anxiously on wet marble tile.

The hot water felt good after their sweaty tryst earlier that evening, and as she waited anxiously for Branch's fantasy to come to life, she found herself enjoying the way the snug black material clung to her drenched, wanton body like a second skin. The whole vibe, she realized, was delightfully claustrophobic. From the encased glass to the pelting hot water to the swirling steam that surrounded her, she felt thoroughly and deliciously isolated from the rest of the world, waiting anxiously in her steam bath for her lover to surprise her with his deliciously twisted and sexy imagination.

Avery might have felt foolish in any other scenario, but here, in this temporary state of utter insanity, standing in the shower in the middle of the night, fully clothed and shivering with desire, made all the sense in her suddenly tipped over, upside-down world.

She felt Branch's presence before she heard him, gently opening the glass door as she turned to find him fully dressed as well. He wore a mischievous, almost embarrassed grin as he hesitated, just for a moment, before stepping in and pulling the door shut behind him.

The click of the latch, slight as it was, sent a shockwave through her body that the hot spray of water first hitting her skin hadn't. She slid gently to one side, reaching out and dragging him closer, until they were both fidgeting anxiously under the spray, not quite sure what to do next but eagerly awaiting whatever might happen just the same.

The water danced across his soft brown curls, dousing them instantly so that they stuck to his forehead, water drizzling down his copper-colored skin as he blinked in response, full lips suddenly wet as his white cotton shirt stuck to his broad chest, exposing the contours of his lightly rouged nipples and vaguely defined abdomen.

She'd been hesitant to indulge him at first, the idea of showering together—fully clothed—sounding too ridiculous and, at first, not very sexy at all. Thoughts of wrinkles and permanent press danced through her skeptical mind. Suddenly, however, she saw the attraction. The sight of Branch Asher—long, lean, and wet, big hands reaching for her— made her shiver and bite her lower lip all over again, eager to make this suddenly very spicy fantasy come true.

He drew her close, not passionately, but more intimately, giving her a warm, wet bear hug as the spray doused them both, making her chuckle with nervous, erotic glee as she waited for what might come next.

She went to speak, to ask him about this fantasy, when it had formed and why and what it all meant, but the minute she opened her mouth, he covered it with his own, shower water and hot, wet desire merging to silence her immediately as the swirl of the steam and the heat of her desire threatened to drown her completely.

His hands clasped either side of her face, big and warm, making her breathless even as his lips released her and those same hands drifted gently onto her shoulders. They danced along her shoulder blades, dragging the thin spaghetti straps of her dress down deliciously until they rested just so on either bicep. They were vaguely binding, keeping her arms at her sides as she remained trapped in place in more ways than one.

He drank her in, skin wet and pebbled with goosebumps as he favored her collarbones with mesmerized kisses, keeping her in place with a vice-like grip on either arm. Gradually he danced them from beneath the watery spray, the glass walls of the spacious shower stall steaming up with the combined heat of the luxuriant mist and their bodies merging in the confined space.

She anxiously waited as he gently began stripping the dress from her torso and down toward her waist like a banana peel, inch by inch, revealing the crests of her pale, pert breasts, and her nipples, stiff and literally begging for attention. He gave them that and more, slathering her with kisses as her body responded in kind, shivering under his eager attention as the hot water spray added a layer of eroticism that she hadn't fully expected but now eagerly savored.

How had she never tried this before?

She'd had no shortage of lovers over the years, God knew, but none had ever worshiped Avery's body the way Branch did in these most tender, intimate moments. While several of her lovers had at least attempted foreplay before diving into home base for a quick bump and grind, she'd always felt it was offered as a mere courtesy, something they felt they were supposed to do rather than something they really *wanted* to do.

Branch was so different as to almost seem from another

species. There was no sense of duty or chore about his min-
istrations, no rushing or impatience as if he couldn't wait to
get to the *good* stuff.

He lingered, he savored, he murmured as if knowing the
longer he took to get there, the better it would be for both of
them. He knew just where to touch her, how long to tease,
how gently to kiss or lick or nuzzle before tweaking or pinch-
ing or even nibbling her into a lathered frenzy.

He did so now, her nipples stiff as his tongue and lips
bathed them with rapt attention, merging with the pebbly
shower spray to drench them completely. At last his hands
began to drag the dress the rest of the way down her body,
drifting past her quivering belly and down her shaking legs.
He traced the outline of its path with his fingertips, pausing
as she stepped out of the dress completely with a hand on either hip to steady her.

Arms free from her sides, she struggled to reach for his top
button when he stopped her with a gentle shake of his head,
a mirthful grin on his lips. She compliantly nodded and
watched as his fingers slid inside her panties to drift straight
to the nuclear heat that had been building between her wet,
sticky thighs ever since they'd left *Papa Pepperoni's.*

Chapter Sixteen: Branch

"Branch! Jesus! God!"

He buried the sound of her passionate outcry with a kiss, covering her lips with his own even as his fingers slid deftly across her aching bud and just inside.

The heat from her desperate pussy was intense, far hotter than the sweltering spray that coated their bodies as he gently pressed her bare back against the steamy shower stall. She gasped at the gentle movement, dragging her lips from his own if only to gulp and croak a murmured curse as his fingers slid gently inside her to mine the sweet, slathered heat between her legs.

She slid her arms around his neck, drawing him closer even as he began to mimic the sensation of himself thrusting, gently, persistently inside her. She ground her swollen mound against the crook of his fingers and thumb, mining them greedily for her first, powerful climax of the night. She bucked, body tensing, and breath rushing into his ear where her cheek rested on his left shoulder.

Branch knew the feeling. Inside his pants, wet and sagging from his lean waist, his own excitement grew with every involuntary gasp and appreciative whimper in his ear. Still, he continued to mine more moans, murmurs, gasps, and bucks as Avery made good use of his hand while her body slithered and squirmed back against the squeaking, steamy glass.

When she had finally had her fill, Avery slid backward, releasing him even as her hands made quick work of his dripping cotton dress shirt and khaki shorts.

She paused, briefs straddling his ankles, to grip and stroke his sensitive prick, the hot water and her eager grip making quick work of whatever resolve he might have had left. Both of them panting, she guided him gently toward her, playfully rubbing his swollen, throbbing tip against her own bud before guiding him just as greedily inside.

They both gasped in unison, a testament to their shared ecstasy as he gripped her waist and, aided by a thigh tightly clutching either side of his hips, began to thrust and pin her against the shower glass in a slow, gentle grind.

Arms wrapped around his neck, legs wrapped around his waist, ass pinned and bouncing against the glass in a most delicious rhythm, Avery gradually took control, guiding their progress, faster, slower, hotter, softer, as Branch responded in kind, pushing when she pulled, grunting as she gasped, belly coiled like a python until he plunged his deepest.

Avery gasped, throbbing as she climaxed and gasping with release. Branch came in kind, bucking and pulsing as their bodies trembled and shivered as one. He held her there, bare back to the steamy shower glass, spray coating their feet as the tremors of their momentous climax murmured and seized and slowed to a dull, pleasant throb.

Inch by inch, she extracted herself from his grasp, planting her feet as they disentangled with a sticky, sweaty sound that made them blush and chuckle nervously, despite the shared intimacy of their current scenario.

He dragged her back under the spray, both of them dancing beneath the swirling mist as the pelting beads of water carried away the sweat and the spunk, if not the desire. He reached for a nearby bar of soap, and with wet, soapy hands, lathered her every nook and cranny and back again. Steady hands and long, tender fingers glided across her feverish, tender skin, under her arms, across her tender nipples, and up and down her thighs, tempting to rouse her libido once more until she grabbed the bar of soap, and before she could pounce on him anew, returned the favor with eager, appreciative hands.

His body glistened under the soapy suds, bare shoulders and swallowing throat and firm chest and trembling belly and bare, dimpled ass as her hands explored every inch of him, eyes flickering from curves to edges and back again until the shower water rinsed him clean and he stood at last, radiant and shimmering in the swirling, sensual steam.

She went to speak, to praise or flatter or perhaps even tease, and he immediately kissed the thought away, burying her girlish flattery with the soft, tender appreciation of his tender kiss. He turned the water off, the sudden silence making room for the sound of blood rushing through her ears, a testament to her still pounding heart.

When they'd toweled each other dry as slowly as they'd lathered each other's writhing, naked bodies, they somehow found the strength to drift onto the bed, warm, soapy bodies nestling one another on the verge of a well-earned nap.

Just before he was about to doze, Avery nudged him with the swell of her ripe, naked rump. "So, where did that particular fantasy come from, stud?"

He snickered playfully, an inch from her ear as they spooned atop the spotless white comforter, his hard body a welcome presence against her soft, curvy hips. "You really want to know?"

Another nudge with her delightfully bare rear that threatened to rouse what was left of his rapidly draining libido. "I asked, didn't I?"

Branch closed his eyes, drifting back six years to the not-so-distant past. "It was the night of the senior dinner," he murmured, breath warm on her still damp neck, hugging her tighter as his hands slid around her naked waist. "We were all supposed to dress up. You wore a little black cocktail dress, emphasis on little. Todd Farmer was a few people in front of you and tried to sneak a bottle of booze in with him and got caught, remember? So there was a holdup at the door while Principal Marchman gave him the *what for* with one of his long-winded speeches, and midway through, it started raining. All your other girly girlfriends ran off to save their dresses, but you just stood in line, waiting and getting wetter and wetter, and I really admired you for that. I thought then maybe you weren't such a snooty-toot, rich girl after all. And I . . . just thought, how nice it would be if the world fell away and no one else was around, and I could go up to you and, you know . . ."

"Tear my dress off in the rain?" Avery teased, her voice a low, subtle murmur as she wriggled deeper into his embrace as sleep threatened to overtake them both.

"Sure, I mean, something like that . . ."

"Well," she purred, gently going slack in his arms. "I guess it's the thought that counts . . ."

He smiled, feeling her breathing slow and thicken until, eventually, soft, gentle snores drifted from the sultry, silken body nestled tightly against his own.

"I've only thought of you every day since, Avery," he murmured to himself just before he, too, drifted into the easiest sleep of his life.

Chapter Seventeen: Avery

"You sexy bastard . . ."

Avery's voice was low and thick, stirring sleepily up from the fog of her slumber and struggling to focus on the glowing phone in her hand.

"Beg pardon?" Her father's voice was equally low and thick, and unless she was imagining things, slightly bemused.

"Oh, shit, sorry, I . . ."

She righted herself, glad it wasn't a video call, and struggling to cover her dewy, besotted skin with a pillow all the same, as if her stepfather could peer straight across the country and see her splayed out like some Vegas hooker on the damp and sweaty bedsheets. "I thought you were someone else."

Branch, that was.

Clearly.

The sun streamed through the blinds, alighting on her still feverish skin, his side of the bed empty and tousled, not another sound in the house but the phone bleating as she struggled to sit upright, her entire body sore from another round of fantasy role play that had left her limbs sore and her throat hoarse.

"Obviously, dear. No wonder you've been ignoring my texts and emails all weekend."

Avery roused herself, standing from the bed and grabbing a silken robe she'd seen hanging from the back of the bedroom door. Padding through the empty house, hoping to find Branch waiting for her in the kitchen, bare ass and holding a steaming coffee mug in her general direction, she murmured disappointedly when neither such fantasy materialized.

"All weekend? I just got here, Dad."

"Clearly, you've had plenty of time in town to seal the deal with some *sexy bastard*, as you so recently put it, Avery."

She chuckled wryly, stumbling through the machinations of brewing herself a pot of coffee despite the fog still clinging to her muddled brain. She held a shiny silver bag of rich, savory grounds in her hand, smirking playfully to herself. "You know, Dad, if you'd wanted me to seal this deal in twenty-four hours or less, why'd you stock the fridge with so many tempting delicacies?"

A low growl introduced her stepfather's epic reply. "Yes, darling, like I flew all the way to that pissant town and stocked the fridge myself, shuffling around the *Piggly Wiggly* with a wobbly cart full of bread and cheese and using my half-off coupons at the checkout line. Sounds just like me and not, in fact, the property manager I pay a monthly fee to upgrade the house for potential resale one of these days."

"Over my dead body," Avery murmured, staring at the gurgling coffeemaker as if her life depended on it.

He sighed on the other end of the line, so heavily and wearily she felt it in her very bones. "I know you loved your mother, dear. God knows we both did for a time. But why you insist on keeping that dilapidated old house in the family is beyond me."

"Dilapidated my ass," she barked playfully. "Have you even seen it lately? You wouldn't recognize it."

"That was the point, dear."

Avery watched the last of the coffee sputter and froth into the pot before yanking it free and pouring it into the awaiting mug in her hand. She leaned back against the counter, waiting for it to cool and staring at the model home interior that used to be a cozy, if cluttered, living room. "You could have at least consulted me about the changes, Dad. I might have had some input?"

"Are you not pleased with the final results, dear?"

"I am and . . . I'm not."

Another world-weary sigh as her father, no doubt, sat in his corner office high atop the corporate offices in New York. "Well, we never did see eye to eye on anything much, did we, dear?"

Avery rolled her eyes and sipped the scalding coffee, ignoring the searing pain on her tongue to force-feed the life-saving caffeine straight into her veins. "Only on one thing, Dad."

He sounded sincerely surprised. "Oh? What's that, dear?"

"We both loved Mom, right?"

A long, pregnant pause followed, uncharacteristic for her busy, harried, *let's go, hurry, faster* father. "Yes, we did, dear. I'm . . . I'm hoping that's not why you're taking so long to seal this deal, though."

Avery clucked her tongue. While she would have gladly stayed in the old house the way it was, surrounded by clutter and memories and doodads and knickknacks from her admittedly dysfunctional childhood, her father's solution was to erase all evidence of it entirely. "Hardly, Dad, it's just . . . Branch has built quite the empire here. He's in no hurry to give all that up, obviously."

Stony silence on the other end of the line. It lasted long enough for Avery to hear the telltale buzzes, rings, bleeps, and clicks of his outer office before he eventually responded. "I wouldn't be interested in him if he hadn't, Avery. That's . . . why you're there, remember? I thought you understood that."

"I read the memo, Dad. I understand the assignment. I'm just telling you it's going to be more challenging than we at first anticipated."

More stony silence followed. Avery was suddenly famished, realizing they'd never eaten anything last night. Well, not food, anyway. She found a buttery, flaky croissant in the fridge and nibbled it nervously as her stepfather formed his reply. She wasn't disappointed. "Perhaps I erred in sending you back home, dear. Perhaps you're not up for the challenge."

She rolled her eyes anew. "Maybe this is how you motivate your other department heads, Father, but your penny ante reverse psychology BS isn't going to work on me."

His grizzled chuckle was an unsettling combination of mirth and menace. "No, of course it wouldn't, Avery. Then let me put it this way, this mission, this get, is your audition for the position you were offered before you left Manhattan. Get it, and you're in. Don't get it, and, well . . . you can start from the ground up like every other employee here."

"Or . . . not?"

"Beg pardon?"

Avery smirked, halfway through her cup of coffee but no longer needing it. Suddenly, adrenaline was her fuel source. "All through school, all I heard was that I was being groomed for management. If six years of my life and total devotion to this company isn't enough to garner more than an internship if I fail to bring Branch into the fold, then . . . maybe I'm simply not management material, Father."

"Maybe not," he mused, softening somewhat. "Or maybe you'll surprise yourself."

"I feel like I already am," she murmured, practically to herself.

"Oh, how so?"

She paused the way he had, eyes peering out at the living room just beyond the kitchen nook while not quite seeing it. "I'm just wondering, why the time crunch? If Branch is such a big get, let's finesse him. Let's wine and dine him. Let's bring him out to New York and show him how his themed entertainment eateries will organically fold into Balthazar Broadcasting, right? I mean, that's what we do for every other big whale we're trying to harpoon."

"Obviously, dear, financials are a bit over your head at this point in your so-called career, but . . . you do understand the tax break and other incentives of bringing him into the organization during this year's final quarter and not next year's first quarter?"

Avery gave an aggressively appropriate shrug that she only wished her father could see, minus the half-open silk robe, that was. "If he's so valuable, who cares, Dad? This empire is growing exponentially, and if we simply try to understand each other here, if we just have enough time to move forward in a more natural way, whatever profits we garner from such a mutual relationship would clearly eclipse the tax break from rushing into something in the next twenty-four hours or so, right?"

Her father's laughter in response was hollow and degrading but not entirely unexpected. All the same, it stung less than it might have before she'd been reunited with Branch. Before she'd had his words, sincere and heartfelt, resounding in her ears. Life wasn't predestined, she reasoned while her father wheezed heartily into the other end of the line. Perhaps her future wasn't with the family business, after all.

Perhaps it never had been. And maybe, just maybe, it took reuniting with her childhood crush to put her life, and her family, such as it was, into perspective as well. "Avery, dear, you sound like you studied at *Berkley* with all those bearded, beatnik professors for six years, and not *Brown*. Don't go hippie on me now just because you're in Southern California for the holidays."

She gave a slow, mirthful smirk. "You might have schooled me, *Step*father, but Mom raised me. I can't deny my DNA, humble as it is."

"No, dear, but you can overcome it."

"But what if I don't want to?" She slightly bristled. Her mother might have been many things—flaky, flighty, emotional, detached—but her personality was hardly something to be overcome.

Her father's voice returned to its monotone business default setting. "I suppose, dear, you should have thought of that before you agreed to take the position."

Avery's response was rapid-fire and unrepentant. "I suppose we both should have."

Another pregnant pause allowed Avery to swallow the last of her croissant and wash it down with suddenly lukewarm coffee. "Be that as it may, dear, I would like to stay abreast of your progress throughout this weekend. And as soon as Branch makes his decision, I will expect news either way."

"Of course," was her curt reply.

She waited for some kind of response in turn but instead heard the click and bleat of the call going dead. She smirked and wished for all the word that it had been Branch ringing her up that morning and not her father. And wondered, idly, what that might mean for her suddenly uncertain future.

CHAPTER EIGHTEEN: BRANCH

"Uh, boss?"

Branch winced, wishing for all the world that Spike wasn't such a damn early riser. Or such an exemplary door greeter. Or such a nosy goddam snoopy-snooperson.

"Yes, Spike," he replied as neutrally as possible, smiling through gritted teeth as he awkwardly stood just inside the warehouse door, both hands full and his patience running on empty.

"Forget your passcode?" Spike all but snickered. He looked so damn merry.

Branch stood his ground, holding half his clothes in one hand and a cardboard container from his own *Comix Café* in the other. "No, I just . . . my hands are full, obviously. Uh, a little help please?"

Spike rose slowly — so very slowly — from his rainbow-colored desk chair and smirked the entire way to the lobby door, drinking in every sordid detail with the sharp, vivid blue eyes behind his thick rectangular glasses as he enjoyed every scandal lovin' minute of the process.

"Sure, absolutely, uh . . . which should I grab first? Your coffee or your clump of last night's clothes from whatever illicit rendezvous you're clearly skulking home from?"

"Very funny," Branch murmured, handing over the corrugated recyclable coffee tray without further discussion. As if on cue, another pair of curious footsteps hurried closer toward them.

Jevon appeared in the suddenly crowded vestibule, adding

to the comical mishaps in the funky warehouse lobby and grinning as he sniffed exaggeratedly at the coffee cup like something out of a Saturday morning kids' cartoon.

In trademark fashion, he wore a rumpled tie-dye bucket hat and a thrift store baseball jersey unbuttoned over a ribbed black tank top and looked for all the world like he'd just stepped off the set of a cheap 70s shark movie. All that was missing was a dented canoe and a comically overlong fishing pole, the lure coming unhinged and yanking off his ridiculous hat to a roaring laugh track.

"Do I smell . . . coffee?"

Branch struggled to hide the blush quickly rising above his wrinkled clothes, clotted pubes, and slept-on hair. He'd been hoping for a quick shower and a new outfit by the time anyone showed up for work that day. Instead, he had two lovebirds posing as detectives to contend with. It was, quite literally, the polar opposite of how he'd seen this morning going.

"Yeah, *my* coffee," Branch murmured hopefully as Spike and Jevon made quick work of the spoils of his last-minute visit to the *Comix Café* drive-thru on the way back from Avery's.

"That's funny," Spike teased, already chugging at his half-soy, oat milk, part whip macchiato. "I thought we were a team. What's yours is mine, and what's ours is yours, that kind of thing?"

"Yeah, that's why I bought us all an espresso and a cappuccino machine for the break room, so . . ." He saw that the boys had already divvied up his half-cocked breakfast, tossing the breakfast sliders and tater tots back and forth between themselves like raptors in a *Jurassic Park* movie.

"Forget it," he mumbled, knowing his goose was already cooked before he'd begun struggling with the keypad just outside the warehouse door.

Jevon and Spike toasted a pair of mouthwatering buffalo

chicken and honey biscuit breakfast sliders in unison.

"Already forgotten, boss man." Spike winked and took a savory bite.

"What are you two doing here already, anyway?"

Branch stood, still looking ridiculous in his walk-of-shame outfit, a combo of whatever he'd been able to throw on before he snuck out of Avery's house at the ass crack of dawn and whatever other incriminating undergarments that he'd had left over from the night before.

Spike and Jevon gave each other knowing glances. "Well, we were hoping, since tomorrow's Christmas Eve, we might get off a little early if we came in a little early today."

They gave him matching toothy face emoji grins Branch would have found comical if half his body wasn't covered with dried spunk and Avery's cabernet-tinted lipstick. All the same, inspiration struck, and he grinned at the unexpected prospect of having the warehouse all to himself — well, Avery included — for the foreseeable future.

"You know, boys," he said, clapping each of them on the shoulder as they gobbled up the last of the breakfast that he'd been savoring for three straight miles. "That's actually a *great* idea."

Jevon swallowed with a comical, audible gulp sound. "It is?"

"Yeah," Spike followed, wiping the grease off his lips with a checkered napkin. "It is?"

"It so is," Branch murmured, warming to the idea with each passing moment. Oh, the fantasies the good old warehouse could inspire. Chairs and desks and bean bags and floors aplenty. And so much room for certain, uh . . . activities.

"In fact, Spike, when you're through chewing my meal, can you do an all-employee email blast and let everyone know that, after today's brainstorming session this afternoon, you've all got the rest of the week off. With pay, naturally."

The two shared disbelieving glances. What followed was a torrent of disbelieving murmurs, exciting possibilities, and yammering, clamoring excitement.

"Uh, excuse me?"

"Since when?"

"You mean, all week?"

"Now, is that a business week or a God-given, seven-day week as Mother Nature first intended?"

"Through New Year's?"

"Wait, New Year's Eve? Or New Year's *Day*?"

"No warehouse, period?"

"And pay? Now, are we talking salary pay or holiday hourly pay?"

Branch nodded at the explosion of joint questions, losing track of who was asking what and when and how loud and merely nodding his head until his neck muscles strained with the effort.

"Yes, yes, now . . . quickly, before I change my mind and have us all work overtime the rest of the year, at half-rate."

Spike and Jevon shared a glance. Jevon murmured, giving Branch a good once over in reply. "Looks like someone's already putting in some late-night after-hours, boss."

"Not funny, Jevon."

"No, but your outfit is."

He tugged on the collar—make that the comically up-turned collar—of his powder-blue button-down *Oxford* shirt. "What? I wear this all the time."

"Yeah, like . . . yesterday."

"As in, you wore that same outfit. Yesterday."

"And?" Branch suddenly felt like he was in high school all over again, on the receiving end of a good cafeteria roasting session.

Spike reached out to finger the wrinkly blue elbow for

emphasis. "But you normally don't wear it inside out, Big Guy."

"And looking like you had it balled up inside your bike basket for a week," Jevon added, giving his partner in crime a quick, wink-wink, nudge-nudge motion.

"So I burned the midnight oil on a business deal last night," Branch bluffed. "What of it?"

"Was it for a lingerie company, Branch, because . . ." Jevon held up a pair of balled-up cotton panties from the pile in his hands before he realized what they were, or why they were still so damp, and dropped them onto the warehouse floor.

Branch snatched them up amidst a fresh round of canoodling, whispering, and snickers, a sound that followed him all the way to the back corner of the warehouse and up the spiral staircase in the back.

He glanced down from the wrought iron railing that ran the length of his private loft high atop the warehouse floor. "Keep it up, you two," he lobbed toothlessly, knowing he'd never follow through with it. "And I'll have you both working overtime this week instead of taking it off."

Though their mouths quit yammering, Branch couldn't help but notice the way they rolled their eyes and smirked and gave each other *yeah, right* spooky fingers before he finally turned his back and stepped into his private shower.

He supposed he couldn't blame them. As far as bosses went, Branch supposed he was the world's easiest pushover. Then again, his staff rewarded him with an amazing barrage of output every year, so he couldn't exactly complain.

And besides, he had fantasies to fulfill, after all. He'd take all the good-natured ribbing Spike and Jevon could dish out as long as it meant he could have Avery all to himself through Christmas Eve, and if all worked as planned, New Year's Eve as well.

Chapter Nineteen: Avery

"Avery? Care to join us?"

Branch stood at the head of a small group of employees seated at a trio of round tables in the employee break room at the back of his warehouse. Like everything else in the cavernous building, it was open-air, spacious, slick, and invariably hip, aglow with the tempting colors of glowing soda and snack machines as well as funky retro apple baskets heaped with colorfully wrapped treats atop the clear Plexiglas counter at his back.

"I'm . . . sorry?"

Avery was as startled as she was steadfast in her desire to stay right where she was, lingering and aloof in the very back of the room.

Branch offered that dazzling smile, even while every head in the room turned to gaze at her as she stood, leaning against a wall partition just behind them. He waved a hand toward himself, radiant in a new variation of his vaguely preppy, effortlessly casual work uniform of untucked collar shirt and khaki shorts with topsiders, no socks.

That would have explained how she woke up to an empty bed that morning, Branch off to shower and change before work, fresh from his side hustle as a softcore porn star in her bed for the last forty-eight hours.

"The kids are brainstorming slogans for the marketing campaign to announce the new drive-in movie theater that's to be the latest addition to Vintage Village."

She remained steadfastly put, nodding as she deadpanned,

"Great, I can't wait to hear their input. From right where I stand."

There were casual snickers and half-covered smiles and plenty of seat wriggling as she effortlessly lobbed Branch's casual invitation back to him with a quick, decisive shutdown of her own.

"You'll hear a lot better from up here," he murmured, not so pleadingly this time, his tone decidedly more threatening behind his big, crooked grin. The casual, almost imperceptibly smooth shift between request and command gave her a momentary glimpse into how he had managed to accomplish so much at such a young age. Behind the gentle eyes and crooked grin was a low-key badass getting his way by whatever means necessary, one wink and nudge at a time.

So help her, Avery kind of . . . dug it.

"Besides," he continued mischievously, clearly enjoying himself. "I promised the kids they'd be able to hear from a big city power broker from Balthazar Broadcasting this morning, so . . . we're waiting, right kids?"

A smattering of ironic applause broke out around the cluster of colored plastic tables as Avery rolled her eyes and forced herself to join him at the front of the room. "How nice of you to offer that without, you know, asking me first."

Despite the pushback, or perhaps because of it, Branch looked as though he was enjoying himself immensely. The assembled staff seemed to appreciate the slight increase of tension in the room, as well, not-so-subtly snickering as Avery nudged him with her hip upon arriving at the front of the room.

She hadn't been expecting an audience when he'd texted her to meet him at his office that morning and so had dressed casually in another outfit from her surprisingly well-stocked closet, white linen slacks and a navy blazer over a muted gray camisole.

She noticed a few of the kids at the table in front of them, hipster dudes and hippie chicks, taking in her overdressed presence with varying degrees of appreciation, and she noted a healthy dollop of apprehension.

It mirrored her recent presentation back at Balthazar HQ, but even this room of strangers greeted her more openly, more warmly than her business partners back home. She wondered what that said about her own company, or even her own stepfather.

The leadership styles of her stepdad and Branch, strong though they both were, were so different as to be polar opposites, and she felt vaguely disloyal warming to the jovial, collaborative atmosphere of Asher Enterprises in a most unexpected and welcome way.

Branch gave her a victorious smirk before addressing his minions. "So, I always like to kick these focus groups off with some no-limits, no-guardrails, let-it-all-out brainstorming. In particular, we're looking for the perfect name to draw people into the retro vibe of this venture at a glance, so . . . go!"

He gave a kind of cruise director, drama kid, thumb and forefinger double barrel pistol point at the assembled staff, who shifted nervously before a tall blonde in bell-bottom jeans and a ribbed Rolling Stones tank top said, "What about *Dangerous Drive-In?*"

Branch nodded. "Great idea, Saffron," he murmured, scribbling the title on the whiteboard between himself and Avery at the front of the room. "A little generic, but we're off to a great start."

Saffron rolled her clever blue eyes at Branch's low-key dig even as he gave her a big, noticeably sweet wink. The rapport between boss and employees was obvious and, Avery noted, powerfully beneficial to the kind of open door, any idea goes vibe suddenly circulating in the rambunctiously colorful break room.

"Don't we want to pin this to a particular era?" a Black kid in an ironic Power Rangers t-shirt asked, tugging thoughtfully on his thick soul patch. He sat unnaturally close to the cheeky emo receptionist who'd reintroduced her to Branch the day before. "Like, weren't drive-ins big in the fifties and sixties?"

"They were big in both those decades, Jevon," Branch pointed out. "But also the seventies, so . . . not so sure we can tack on a decade to this one like we did the *Creature Café*, which was predominantly a black and white fifties-themed opportunity designed to appeal specifically to Boomers."

Next to Jevon, Spike straightened his glasses thoughtfully and murmured, "But even as *Creatures Café* evolved, we subtly included different eras as well, right? From black and white monster movies like Frankenstein and the Wolfman to Freddy and Jason, so . . ."

The kids all murmured in unison, not quite conferring with each other as much as they were *near* each other, each of them muttering as if to themselves. A twiggy ginger girl in a crooked trucker cap and, well, not much else offered, "We have the *Decades Disco*, so we *have* done something about an era without actually naming the era."

"Facts, Marigold," Branch said, nodding as if this were quite the revelation. "So maybe we should start thinking of an era, or a feeling, or what connotes a drive-in for most people so that we steer away from pinning this to a particular decade."

Suddenly, the room crackled to life with a cacophony of feedback from everyone, everywhere, all at the same time.

"Well, we've never actually been to one, Branch—"

"Or seen one—"

"Or know what the hell you're talking about, so . . ."

Chuckles all around. Eye rolls aplenty. Hip checks. Ribcage nudges. Snickers galore.

"How about a . . . disco?"

The chuckles stopped as, one by one, each head turned toward Avery, each pair of eyes tinged with a veil of scrutiny. She felt like she'd just stepped into a black and white western movie, the lone stranger walking through those swinging doors into the local saloon, every cowpoke and barmaid and sheriff and outlaw in town giving her the evil eye as the swinging doors kicked her backside one by one and forced her to tumble even deeper into the intimidating environment.

She ignored them eagerly, having seen far worse in nearly every staff meeting back at Balthazar Broadcasting HQ, a far more hostile work environment she'd been navigating since about the same age as the late teens-slash-early twenty-somethings seated before her. "I mean, have you guys seen one of those before?"

Murmurs greeted her sudden interjection. "Probably not," she muttered before inching a little closer to the assembled crowd. "And yet *Decades Disco* literally rolls off the tongue."

The kids seemed surprised there was a compliment attached to that particularly abrupt interjection. "Roller rinks?" she continued, stalking up and down the cluster of funky, modern, hipster breakroom tables, each pair of curious eyes following her pantherlike progress as she paced menacingly up and down. "Those were before your time, too, and yet? And yet you all came up with *Retro Rink*? That's some classic, chefs kiss, ten-out-of-ten branding right there."

More murmurs, even more nods, and quite a few smiles graced the young, curious, even skeptical faces following her back-and-forth progress like spectators at a tennis match.

"So a drive-in shouldn't be any problem for this particular brain trust, right guys?" Avery found herself adopting the same kind of carnival barker, camp counselor tone Branch had when addressing the team assembled before her. They squirmed, half-confused as to whether she was still complimenting them or not.

"So, what do you suggest?"

Avery glanced back at Saffron, the blonde in the trucker cap. She cocked her head and glanced back before offering wryly, "You're the ivy league hot shot, Avery. What do *you* suggest?"

Avery's response was quick, subtle, and laced with a hefty dose of city girl attitude, her voice as gritty as the glint of steel in her eyes. "I thought you kids ran the show around here."

Saffron smirked as others chuckled. Branch offered, "As you may have guessed by now, we're pretty casual here, Avery. Anyone can weigh in at any time, so . . . any ideas?"

Avery shrugged, giving the room a softly knowing grin. It was, she suddenly realized, Branch's subtle way of handing the meeting over to her. "Given my limited experience with drive-in movie theaters, so . . . wait? Is this an actual drive-in or like a diner with a drive-in vibe?"

Branch regarded her curiously, in a different, more personal way than he had all weekend. Even when he glanced up at her from between her legs in her very own kitchen. "It's . . . a real drive-in theater. Ticket booth, concession stand, giant digital screen, hundreds of parking spots, picnic tables, servers on roller skates running around with craft cocktails, fresh, gourmet flavored popcorn, and other artisanal treats . . ."

She couldn't contain her excitement. "Really? Cool! That . . . that's a really rad idea, actually."

The room laughed as one, a not-unpleasant sound nor, Avery surmised, an unpleasant development. She ignored their good-natured ribbing, instinctively sensing that they were laughing *with* her and not, for once, at her. She marveled at how good that made her feel, how positive of a vibe Branch had created out of such an outwardly bland, boxy workspace.

She responded accordingly, leaning into the question not

with a softball response but with the same level of enthusiasm as everyone else in the room. Suddenly, inexplicably, she was rooting for Branch's next venture to succeed in a very big way.

"So, I mean, if that's the case and this is a big, wide movie screen in the middle of a field, the title should hint at what an awesome, one-of-a-kind, uniquely unheard of anymore experience this is. I mean, so bizarre, you drive your car and park and watch a movie in your car, and literally no one in this room has done that before, and chances are lots of others in your target audience haven't either, so we should try to communicate that in the concept art as well as tag lines and other ancillaries, so the metrics and deliverables should reflect the more . . ."

Avery felt the vibe in the warehouse dampen as she slowed her spiel to a crawl. Glancing out at a sea of blank, young faces, she turned to find Branch grinning from ear to ear. "Not all of us went to *Brown* for their MBA, Avery. Not all of us went to college at all. Most of us are homegrown hustlers, so . . . in English, please?"

Avery chuckled, forgetting herself. "I, okay, well, for instance . . ." She turned to the whiteboard, snatching the dry-erase marker from a grinning Branch and starting to brainstorm a few possibilities in her typically frenetic style.

"So, let's say you focus on what made drive-ins famous back in their heyday, which was basically science fiction movies with giant ants and grasshoppers or alien invasions or *The Blob*, for instance, so you could play off the Sci-Fi Cinema aspect and expand that into your marketing language, with terms like *creature comfort* and *campy cocktails* and *monster size screen* and *snacks from another dimension,* etc."

Avery felt an energy shift in the room and turned to find many of Branch's *kids* squirming in their seats. "What about non-science fiction movies that play there, though?"

She nodded, still riffing. "I assume this is an artisan market, right, Branch? I mean, you'll be running older films you get from independent companies, not a Friday national release scenario? I know there are a lot of politics involved in film distribution, but the indie rental market is still pretty affordable. This lets you pick and choose not only what movies you want to play but which genres of film. So, for instance, you can do *Dangerous Double Features* with back-to-back action movies and still, vaguely, stay under the Sci-Fi Cinema banner and . . . Jevon, a question?"

"How about chick flicks?"

On either side of him, Marigold and Saffron each playfully punched an arm. Beside him, Spike mischievously and dramatically distanced himself before he, too, got canceled along with his significant other. "What? Action movies can't be chick flicks?" Marigold asked.

"Or movies with robots?" Saffron seconded.

"Or monster movies?" Avery chided good-naturedly as she waved the dry-erase playfully toward a mock-cowering Jevon. As more questions and answers began to fill the room, Avery took a glance from scribbling them on the dry-erase board to find Branch admiring her with a curious expression that was almost as sexy as his usual come hither gaze.

Too bad the kids had too many ideas for her to return the curious glance before she returned to the whiteboard instead, struggling to keep up with the sudden flood of youthful inspiration.

Chapter Twenty: Branch

"Is every day like this?"

Branch turned from the soda machine, a cold, frosty can in either hand as he returned to one of the recently vacated break room tables at the back of the warehouse.

"Not really," he explained, sliding the grape soda over toward Avery's side of the freshly delivered pizza box in the middle of the purple plastic table. "We all know each other pretty well by now, so we really let the fur fly when it's time for a brainstorming session. The kids were pretty reserved today since you're new."

Avery seemed just a little more than surprised. "That was the kids being . . . reserved?"

Branch grinned, still so surprised by the recent turn of events he couldn't help himself. "Pretty much, yeah. What? They don't riff like that up in your Ivory Tower overlooking Central Park?"

She frowned and flipped open the pizza box, launching a burst of mozzarella, spinach, and olive flavor into the otherwise stale warehouse atmosphere.

"First of all, it's not an Ivory Tower, and second of all, that's the first time I've been able to conduct a brainstorming session without being drowned out by mansplaining from ninety percent of the assholes in the room, so . . . I think we can both agree today was a landmark victory for *moi!*"

Branch nodded in unreserved agreement. "You definitely were a hit, Avery."

"*We* were a hit," she reminded him, waving a piece of pizza she'd curled expertly as steam swirled from its drizzled, melty goodness.

"We do make a good team," he murmured, forming an entirely new fantasy he'd never allowed himself to imagine before. He glanced her way, wondering if she was really savoring her pizza so much that she had to close her eyes and murmur appreciate *mmmm's* and *yummo's* or was just avoiding the topic altogether. Branch was no dummy. He figured it was a little bit of both.

He shrugged and dug in, suddenly famished after the last official workday of the holiday season. The pizza was hot and fresh, and as he finished his first slice, she tapped the top of the box with a greasy finger.

"*Dashing Delivery*?" she mused, reading the box top before opening it to reach for another slice. "Sounds like something you and the kids cooked up."

"Three of them at various ends of town," he murmured, grabbing a slice before the top could drift back down again. "Closest thing I've got to a chain in Lakemont."

She nodded, wearing a bemused expression as sexy as anything he'd ever seen before. "Do you ever sleep?"

"Sure, I mean, a few hours a night. When my crazy brain lets me shut down long enough, that is."

Avery glanced around, looking elegant but approachable in her dressy casual attire. "Where, Branch? I feel like all we've done is bounce from here over to my place and back to here."

He nodded at a small spiral staircase in the far corner of the warehouse, following Avery's eyes as she glanced up at the wraparound loft on the second floor.

Their eyes met across the red and white striped pizza box. "You sleep here?"

"Yeah, I mean . . . that way, I'm always up and ready to get started when inspiration strikes."

"You don't have a home?"

He hedged. "I have a few in town, but they're mainly investments, rentals, that kind of thing." He glanced around the warehouse, silent now, the kids all gone for winter break, the cavernous space housing just the two of them at the moment. "I like it here. Honestly, I could live anywhere in town, but every time I tried to move out and settle down, I kept coming right back here. No place . . . nowhere else feels like home to me."

She wriggled deeper into her molded turquoise seat, smiling contentedly. "I can see why. You've created quite the world for yourself here, Branch."

"Well, I've had a lot of help."

"Sure, but . . . you did all this, all of it, by yourself. That's quite an achievement." She seemed to be looking around the warehouse, up and down and in between, before glancing back at him with a curious expression.

"Everything I have was already built by someone else," she confessed.

Branch inched forward in his seat. "Not everything, Avery. You earned that MBA all by yourself."

She rolled her eyes. "Please, I could have slept through every class, and they would have given me a four-point-oh GPA based on my last name alone."

"I can't imagine you sleeping through a single class, Avery. You love learning too much."

"A lot of good that's going to do me now."

He sat back, waving his orange soda can absently. In all the time he'd known her, watched her, observed her, Branch had never seen Avery this . . . disillusioned. "You know, Avery, your future's not written in the stars."

Her glance back was futile at best. "It . . . kind of is, Branch. I mean, I've been groomed all my life since the day Dad boarded my mother's flight and whisked her off her feet and into his very private, very exclusive world." She paused, glancing over at him. "What? What's that look for?"

"I just, you're such a smart person, and you're talking like an indentured servant. You weren't born just to further your stepfather's insanely ambitious legacy. You were born to live your own life. If you want to run Balthazar Broadcasting because *you* want to run it, that's one thing. If you just feel you have to because there's no one else in the family to do it, that's . . . not a life. That's a . . . a . . . life sentence."

She clucked her tongue and rolled her eyes, but those eyes were moist and vulnerable just the same when they met his across the crowded break room table. "You do have a way with words, Branch. I'll give you that much."

"I just . . . care about you, Avery. I always have. Even . . . even when it was just from afar. And I guess whatever this thing is between us that's been going on this weekend has given me the opportunity to say and do things I never could before."

She wriggled lower in her seat, gaze suddenly sultry as if she wanted to leave reality far, far behind.

He supposed he couldn't blame her, though he felt sad that her reality was something she needed to escape from so badly in the first place. All the same, he was more than willing to help her do just that.

"So, I've been dying to ask all day, are there . . . any more fantasies you'd care to indulge in before you hear my pitch tomorrow?"

He chuckled, vaguely embarrassed. "Well, we kind of already are . . ." He waved his hand around the break room, settling on their cozy plastic funky table for two.

"This is a fantasy?"

"It was for me for a long time. Back in school. Every Friday was pizza day, remember?"

She made a very Avery-like face, stiff and eye-rolling and

superior. "Those square things that felt like cardboard and tasted even worse? Don't remind me."

"It wasn't the taste I remember, Avery. It was sitting in the cafeteria, watching you and your friends eating pizza. And drinking . . ."

He let his eyes wander to the soda in her hand. She noticed, following suit. Smiling, wide and big and quick and sudden. The very sight warmed his belly and, well . . . elsewhere. "Grape soda. You . . . remembered?"

He gave her a superior *tut-tut* of his own. "Of course I did, Avery."

She savored another sip, putting on a big show with those full, suddenly damp lips. Those wet, plump, kissable lips. "God, I haven't tasted one of these in years."

"Is it as good as you remember?" Branch struggled to comprehend a world where grape soda wasn't an integral part of someone's daily diet. Then again, maybe Avery was right after all. Maybe spending so much time with kids fresh out of high school or still going to college had him stuck in a perpetual youth of his own.

Then again, it had worked pretty well for him so far.

Avery shrugged and set the can down. Beneath the table, she had kicked off one of her sandals and slid her bare feet atop his shin. "You may not believe me when I say this, Branch, but you've made this unexpected trip down Memory Lane better than anything I can remember."

He winked, pressing his shin into the warmth of her toes and fighting the urge not to melt into a puddle of goo and slip beneath the table like some gelatinous mass. "That's good, Avery, because . . . we're just getting started."

She made a very different kind of *O* face. "Oh yeah?"

"Sure, I mean, this isn't the only fantasy I have left."

She wagged a playful finger, sliding her foot away and abruptly standing. He watched her rise to her full height, statuesque and shapely in her sexy suit. "Oh no, big guy. You just wasted your fantasy on pizza and grape soda. It's my turn now."

CHAPTER TWENTY-ONE: AVERY

"You can come in now..." Avery murmured coyly, squirming beneath the soft white covers as Branch opened the bedroom door wearing a curious expression, and ... not much else.

He drank her in, surveying the outline of her body splayed provocatively beneath the single white sheet as if committing it to memory. "I feel ridiculous," he said, nodding down at the thin, powder-blue towel wrapped around his waist.

"You don't look it, Branch, trust me."

Avery admired his long, boyish form, smooth, handsome, and lean, and for the rest of the night, hers and hers alone. The very thought made her practically wanton with desire. Mad, uncontrollable, unfamiliar desire.

As much as she enjoyed the time they spent together, uh ... fantasizing, Avery enjoyed the sheer, panty-drenching thrill of anticipating what might happen next. It was her mind's way of enjoying foreplay before the foreplay, and she had come to savor the mere thought of his touch as much as she did his actual touch.

He nodded her way, appreciating the way her pert nipples made tiny tents beneath the clingy white bedsheet as she lay, propped gently up on the pillows gathered against the wrought iron headboard behind her.

He addressed her staggeringly stiff nipples as he gently murmured, "You, either, hot stuff."

He stood there, still in the doorway, glancing at the minimalist bedroom décor even as she drank in the noticeable bulge threatening beneath his clingy blue towel. "Uh, you said something about a fantasy?"

She nodded at the leather settee across from her bed, wide and inviting. "Sit," she commanded with a playful growl, enjoying the way he did so immediately, no questions asked, like a little boy at the doctor's office. The low light in the bedroom flattered his taut belly and broad shoulders, to say nothing of his lean, curious face and the way the thin towel barely contained the girth of his thickening prick.

He stared back at her, face a mask of curiosity and anticipation. Hers must have looked quite similar as she wriggled higher up in the bed, if only for a better look at his half-naked form and perhaps, to feel the mattress beneath her rasp across her deliciously hypersensitive—and buck-ass naked—skin. She held the sheet tight to her chest, just high enough to tease him with glimpses of her tan lines and the nipples that begged to be released with the slightest tug on the sheet.

He licked his lips, waiting for an explanation.

She gave it . . . kind of. "Did you ever, you know . . . think of me?"

He grinned, a hand tightly gripping the armrests on either side of him. His left foot tapped up and down nervously. She loved that, even after all they'd shared together, even after how many times he'd pleasured her, how often she'd called out his name in sheer ecstasy, he was still nervous about what might come next. "Only all the time, Avery. How many times do I have to tell you that?"

"No, I mean, did you ever really think of me when you, you know . . . pleasured yourself?"

The blush that rose to his clean-shaven cheeks was answer enough, but he sputtered out a reply all the same. "Who . . . who says I pleasured myself? And when? And why? What, I mean . . . why would you say that?"

"Oh my God, all guys do, Branch. Girls, too. Yours truly

does, that's for damn sure. Don't be shy now, after all we've . . . been through together this weekend. I'm just asking if you ever thought of me, pictured me, fantasized about me when you did?"

He glanced away, biting his lower lip as if troubled over how to answer.

"It's okay, Branch," she murmured, squirming beneath the sheets even as her belly trembled with desire and the long distant memory of closing her eyes and seeing him in front of her, much as he was right now. "I always thought of you whenever I, you know . . ."

"Pleasured yourself?"

"Sure, all the time. Every time, actually. You . . . you were my go-to fantasy boy."

"Bullshit."

"Scout's honor, big guy." He still looked doubtful, so she tried a more thorough explanation. "No, really. With your glasses and stupid scary movie t-shirts and pants always dragging down around your waist, I would get home from school and tell myself, *not tonight, Avery*. And then, every night, before I went to sleep, I'd lie in bed and close my eyes and imagine what kind of boxers or briefs you might wear, what your soft, pale skin might taste like, what you'd do if I took your glasses off, or nibbled your earlobe and I'd get all hot and bothered and . . ."

She made a noise, quite unconsciously, reliving the power of those massively titillating and forbidden teenage orgasms so many years ago. And here she was, in the same room with her crush, watching him grow harder beneath his thin blue towel with every low, murmured syllable of her recollection.

"I still call bullshit, Avery." Even as he said the words, Branch still sounded less skeptical this time around.

She nodded convincingly, eyed him so salaciously, and squirmed so . . . suggestively . . . beneath the sheets that

Branch had no choice but to believe her. All the same, he nudged his chin back at her with a cheeky challenge that was reflected in the soft, gently leering look in his eyes. "Show me, then."

"What, now?" Somehow, in all her planning and fantasizing, in all her delicious anticipation, Avery hadn't thought Branch would actually have the balls — no pun intended — to challenge her to pleasure herself first. This . . . this wasn't supposed to be how her fantasy went. And yet, somehow, it seemed almost delightfully better.

He was suddenly cocky, smirking as he sat across from her, nodding at the way she lounged so seductively before him. "Sure. I mean, I assume you're naked under there, right?"

She grew cocky in response, enjoying the back and forth as the temperature inside the room grew by degrees with every sassy, heated exchange. "Says who?"

"Says those *Hershey* kiss nipples of yours standing at attention and that little wet spot steadily growing between your legs, that's who . . ."

She blushed, one hand caressing down across her already trembling belly to feel the warmth, the wet, gooey heat, between her gently spread thighs. "Well, I'll be, Branch. I guess it's true . . . just looking at you makes me wet."

He leaned forward, as if for a better look. His voice, when he finally spoke, was gently commanding. "So . . . show me then."

She might have laughed if her throat wasn't held in a vice-like grip of intense desire. "Hold on, big guy, this is my fantasy we're talking about here!"

"And clearly, you're into it, so . . ."

He sat back in his chair, brash in a way she'd never seen him before. And she was unmistakably, gushingly loving every minute of it. He spread his arms wide. They were wiry, with just a whisper of underarm hair to drive her over the edge. She wriggled back until his thighs gently spread, and she saw just a hint of the bulge beneath.

"But my fantasy is watching you . . . do yourself." Her argument was as weak as her will to deny him what he so clearly wanted.

"Trust me, Avery, I can't wait to touch myself while you're touching yourself, but rules are rules, and . . ."

"These are fantasies, Branch. There are no rules!"

He nodded in her direction. She was surprised to still feel one hand beneath the sheets, gently resting on her feverish mound as if waiting for a signal to begin. As if, she mused, waiting for . . . permission.

"Yeah, well, I'm not starting until you get busy, so . . . we can sit here wanting to touch ourselves all night, or you can get busy getting busy and kick this fantasy into high-gear already."

She grinned at his sudden turning of the tables, from the boyish charm of their first *taste test* of each other to this playfully forceful, nay bossy self. Either way, he was keeping her on her toes. Or, in this case, on her back. Avery found she liked it, surreptitiously beginning to circle her pulsing clit beneath the sheets even as his eyes grew big and he watched her with obvious aplomb.

As Avery gave herself to the moment, she let the sheet fall gently away from her breasts, stiff and tender, as she used her left hand to gently tweak and tease them as she would normally on her own.

Without an audience, of course.

Through heavy-lidded eyes and the veil of self-pleasure, she admired Branch's plump lips and wide, eager eyes. As if knowing he was being watched, he reached slightly forward and with long, tempting fingers, gripped the bottom of the thin white sheet that covered her and gently dragged it down her naked, writhing body.

The slow, purposeful drift of soft white cotton rasping across her skin, deliciously caressing her exposed pores, and fluttering across her taut, shuddering belly, forced a dangerous moan of pleasure from between Avery's gaping lips. As the sheet made its way across her damp landing strip of pubic thatch, she spread her legs salaciously and drizzled two wet, sticky fingers around her throbbing clit, noting the way Branch licked his lips before dragging the sheet off the bed entirely.

She gasped at the release, body bare and splayed out as Branch let his hand drift from the sexy bedsheet and toward his belly. He caressed it, softly, slowly, in little round, teasing motions that drifted lower and lower toward the top of his towel as she watched his own body tremor with pleasure.

As if performing a magic trick, his erection steadily grew and inched the towel up and away, slithering between the flap like a menacing cobra as Branch undid the soft, gentle knot at the top. The towel drifted to either side of his bare hips, his cock stiff and turgid as he continued to wriggle his bare ass deeper into the leather loveseat as he eased into the heat and desire of the moment.

The sight made her gasp, to say nothing of the way she pressed two expert fingers against her gaping clit, writhing beneath her own slippery touch as Branch finally gripped the base of his cock as if to challenge how much eye-candy she could stand in one sitting.

The headboard creaked and moaned behind her as she wriggled for a better view, all the while grinding herself into a lather as she climaxed anew. She savored this raw and unfiltered view at Branch in the buff, cock stiff in his gentle grasp, balls thick and heaving each time he stroked himself almost absently, his hungry eyes literally feasting on every detail of the rich landscape between Avery's eagerly spread thighs.

She smiled, satisfied with herself but not completely. After all, she hadn't shared every detail of her fantasy with Branch, which always ended very differently than the way it began. Finishing off another thigh-clenching orgasm, Avery shook her head with resolve and, on wobbly legs, rose to greet the second half of her long-buried dream.

CHAPTER TWENTY-TWO: BRANCH

"Keep going," Avery murmured, bare feet on the hardwood floor beneath her even as she panted from the effort of her latest gushing climax.

Branch nodded, if only to get a better view of Avery's supple, naked form, glistening with sweat — and more — as she sat on the edge of the bed before him. She was resplendent, bare skin aglow, nipples taut, and eyes hungry as she drank him in, inch by steady inch. He felt seen and wanted in a way he never had before.

He swallowed, nodding down at the way he stroked himself lazily as her eyes followed up and down his throbbing, leaking cock. "Is this . . . what you always wanted?"

She nodded, biting her lower lip coyly as she gripped each one of his knees with a different hand. They were warm to the touch and sticky from her efforts, like the dappled dew on her belly and the glossy sheen on her slim strip of rich, dark pubic thatch, damp now, like the rest of her softly quaking body.

She nodded again, swallowing hard as their eyes finally met across the desperate few inches that still separated them. "It's so much more, Branch."

Her voice was guttural, sending shivers through his already leaking prick even as her hands crept gently up his thighs as if to intensify his already uncontrollable craving for everything Avery.

His skin was on fire, and hers was as well. Every sizzle of her fingertips sent tremors through his body, tempting his eyes to roll back into his head and his cock to erupt with a shuddering, if premature, orgasm. He struggled to control himself, even as his belly threatened to heave and shudder with a mind of its own.

He had felt foolish at first, eager with excitement, growing beneath his towel, embarrassed at the thought of stroking himself in front of Avery, of all people. He could barely admit to jerking off in the first place. Now, he had to give proof of how he actually did it? He had never been an exhibitionist before, and even after all they'd shared so far, Branch was still hesitant to pleasure himself in the presence of another living soul.

It had almost . . . almost . . . been a deal breaker.

But at the first sign of her fingers drifting gently beneath the sheets, moving expertly around her own glistening bud, Branch had lost all inhibition and eagerly leaned into her lurid fantasy with gusto.

Watching his longtime crush pleasure herself, her flushed face a mask of ecstasy, thighs spread and pussy glossy and pink with wet desire, was a gift he never expected to receive.

As he continued to admire her naked form, hair sticking to her sweaty shoulders, nipples still puffy and pink, her knees touching his as she sat on the edge of the bed across from him, her hands made the last of the journey up his thighs to greet his shivering loins. One palm slid low to cup his eager balls while the other joined his at the base of his desperate shaft.

Avery squeezed it for emphasis, winking saucily. "I'll take it from here, big guy," she murmured as his own hands drifted away to grip the big leather chair's armrests once more. She stroked him until the mattress squeaked with her departure, and she stood, only to slither onto his thighs with her own.

He gasped with surprise and the approach of a staggering release that he could already feel throbbing deep inside. She gripped his hands atop the armrests, inching closer to his throbbing cock with her slick, pink lips until they met, caressing his veiny shaft as if meant for that very purpose. She slathered him with her heat and musk, gripping him tightly between her slick, thick lips and grinding up and down but never onto his straining erection.

Faster, wetter, and longer, hands gripping his and flesh gripping flesh until he grunted and thrust one last time. He coated both their bellies and chests with a blast of untethered spunk that thrilled them both with nervous laughter.

As if one-upping him in the O-face department, Avery slid slightly forward and used the last of his throbbing erection to grind, press, and wriggle her way to release. He got the hint, wrapping his arms around her slippery waist to draw her closer. And with the last of his staggering hard-on, pressed against her aching clit until she began to grip and moan her way into one last lip-biting, pussy throbbing orgasm.

When her lust was sated and his passion dwindled, she sank onto his chest, heart pounding as her arms instinctively wormed around his neck to draw him into an achingly tight embrace.

"Thank you," she murmured, almost tearfully, as her warm breath oozed across his left ear and their chests pounded against one another's. "Thank you for . . . everything."

He had so much to say, so many things he wanted to convey, but instinctively Branch knew that now was not the time. Instead, he simply held her until her bear hug softened, and then, and only then, did he help her into bed just before they both drifted off to another sweaty, steamy nap.

CHAPTER TWENTY-THREE: AVERY

"Mmmmmmm . . ."

Avery woke gradually, body pleasantly sore after their dinnertime tryst. An involuntary smile teased the corners of her lips as she wriggled deeper into the mattress, wanting nothing more than to keep her eyes shut and relive the thought of Branch, legs spread before her, member in hand and stroking himself to the gentle rhythm of his smooth, dancing balls.

As if on cue, she felt another presence in the room. No, not just in her room—in her bed. Warm and smooth and dense and still practically steaming from their sizzling sexcapades. She turned her head, slightly, to find Branch lying next to her, eyes gently shut, lips slightly parted, bare chest rising and falling slowly, still in the grips of sleep as she had been only moments earlier.

Part of her wanted to drift right back into dreamland with fantasies and images anew to flood the back of her eyelids with lurid, lustful imagery as she blushed her way through another wet dream. Or, perhaps, to rest and recuperate for what might happen next—and how often. She struggled against the temptation and realized that a new fantasy was sleeping right next to her, and to waste it would be a sin in and of itself.

She gently turned until she was on her side and facing him. The bedsheet was still coiled half off the bed, half on the bedroom floor. The curtains were still open, bright moonlight bathing Branch's softly naked body in a most flattering way as her breath caught in her throat, taking in his effortless splendor, and hardly believing her good fortune.

She drank him in eagerly, every quiet, sleeping inch. His ruddy brown curls were still damp from the intensity of their passionate coupling only hours earlier. His gently flaring nostrils and ripe, kissable lips were viewed in outline with his head slightly turned toward the window.

His skin was taut and smooth, arms at his side, belly so flat it was almost concave above the gently smattered happy trail of dark brown hair leading from his belly button down into his thickly natural thatch of curly dark pubes. His manhood, even while flaccid, lay long and curved and rosy-pink against one leg, gently crooked at the knee while the other was so long his foot hung off the edge of the bed.

Avery, drowsy enough to drift right back to sleep only a moment ago, was fully awake, her senses alive and on overdrive as she found her heart pounding anew. She had no idea what time it was, but judging by the dampness still clinging to her legs and the gently wet spot on Branch's softly breathing belly, they'd only been asleep a short while. All the same, she knew there would be no sleep again for her that night until she satisfied herself once more.

She smiled greedily, alone in the dark, staring at Branch in the altogether even as her heart began to race anew. She realized her time with him was growing short. She also knew that her father had been right. If he didn't go for her pitch the next night, there would be no reason for her to stay past Christmas.

She would have to return to home base, hat in hand, tail between her legs, only to admit to her father that her secret mission had failed. The knowledge, cold and dead like a weight in her belly, only made her want to use the time they had left to her full advantage.

She hadn't been expecting a reunion with Branch in the first place, let alone a seventy-two-hour sex-a-thon full of each and every one of their lurid teenage fantasies, and even a few formed off the cuff and on the fly. Now that she was so deeply embedded in this strange erotic netherworld, she wanted to savor every nook and cranny of Branch's youthful, unspoiled body for as long as she could—and for as long as he could take it.

Tentatively, so as not to wake him, she let her fingertips drift along the still damp curls nearest her. They were soft, moist, and splendid, drifting back into place as soon as her finger slid gently away.

Her frosted nail tips glowed in the pale moonlight, as did the softly glowing expanse of Branch's quietly naked body, still breathing heavily, his eyes wide shut. Avery risked a glance of one softly caressing fingertip along his jawline. Softly, barely touching but still feeling the warmth of his smooth skin all the same. When he still didn't rouse, she inched closer, finger dancing to caress his lower lip and trace its every plump twist and curve.

He stirred suddenly. She froze her finger in place. His eyes opened, and winking saucily, he opened his mouth so quickly she couldn't pull away before he wrapped his lips around her eager fingertip, surrounding it with wet, titillating heat that instantly had her in the throes of a fresh, new fantasy to behold.

"Mmmmmm," he murmured, sucking so eagerly she clearly had no choice but to let him. To deny him would have been rude, after all, and truth be told, she couldn't have even if she'd tried. The sensation was daring and new, instantly seizing her in the grip of another frantic, heart-pounding panic. When she managed to slither her finger, wet down to the base, from between his tightly clenched lips, he frowned and turned his face toward hers.

"I've been waiting for you to wake up, Avery."

"Really?"

He sighed, gently exhaling as he nodded and smiled his gentle, crooked smile. "Just lying here in the dark, willing you to wake up and find me here, still in your bed."

She smiled, squirming at the thought. "For how long?"

"Long enough to want you again," he murmured, stretching his arms above his head as she watched his naked body stretch out and down like life-size taffy. "So, a few minutes at least."

She rolled her eyes and in so doing, saw that he wasn't kidding; he really *did* want her again. Or at least, the stiffening prick dancing along his happy trail sure did. She watched it slither and pulse back to life, savoring every inch and tasting its meaty, sultry heft in her memory.

"I'm surprised you could wait that long," she purred seductively, her fingertip still wet from his mouth as it drizzled down his ribcage. Branch shivered with an audible murmur, reaching up and sliding his hands beneath the back of his neck with a satisfied, almost swaggering grin.

He had to know how good he looked to her at that very moment, how badly she wanted him, even craved him, his naked body bathed in the moonlight and just lying there, waiting to be explored.

"Then again," she murmured, dancing her trail of slickness down the veiny ridge of his growing hard-on and savoring every meaty inch with the tender sensations of her drizzling fingertip. "I can hardly wait myself."

"Great minds think alike," he murmured, glancing at her with that shit-eating grin even as she grew dazzled by his ebullient smile.

"Yeah, only I'm tired of just thinking about it."

"Yeah, me, too."

His voice was slow and steady, as if he already knew what she wanted to do—and how badly she wanted to do it. Her voice was just above a whisper, murmuring gently in his ear as they both watched her lazily slither her single fingertip up and down the length of his stiffening staff. He murmured quietly, squirmed gently, and pinned her gaze with his own.

"I never want to leave this bedroom, Avery."

She chuckled coyly, flattered and nodding at the same time. "Who says we have to?"

"I mean, we'll have to come up for air sometime, I suppose."

"Who needs to breathe, Branch? I can hardly breathe when I'm around you anyway."

He smiled, nodding. "Same here, but . . . we'd have to eat eventually, I suppose."

She squeezed him playfully, holding him in place and watching the pleasure ooze across his face like syrup spreading across a steaming plate of fresh flapjacks. "I've got everything I need right here, big boy," she murmured, nibbling his earlobe for emphasis before winking and slithering gently down the bed.

One quick downward motion, a slight adjustment of her belly and hips, and she was there—right there, greedily sucking the rigid cock throbbing between his legs. There was no hesitance this time, no shyness or reservations as Avery's lust awakened with a dizzying force that she knew better than to try and resist.

She gorged herself on his prick, savoring the way it was still peppered with his earlier drizzle of eager spunk and licking him clean as her eyelids fluttered with unbridled lust. He was so hot and stiff between her lips, so eager and thrusting as she slathered him from tip to base and back again, feasting as if truly savoring a gourmet meal.

Raucous sounds filled the room, joining with his murmurs and her moans as she eagerly slid more and more of him inside her hungry lips until he gasped and thrust gently, as greedy as she was horny, as hungry as she was ready.

She pulled back slightly, gently spreading his pale, endless thighs as she repositioned herself before eagerly encasing him in her tightly gripping lips, nose tickled by his damp thatch and lips glancing along the savory, warm flesh at the base of his staff.

Still spread out, arms behind his head and gently gripping the wrought iron bed post for traction, he pumped and thrust in reply, sliding between her appreciative lips as if it were a dress rehearsal for the mercifully blissful pounding yet to come.

She gave in willingly, bawdy, and greedy between his legs until he shifted his weight gently away and slipped gradually from within her mouth's velvet clutches. He leaned forward to grip her face between his big hands, favoring her with a gently probing kiss as curious as it was surprising, as if mining her very lips to freely taste of himself there.

When he finally let her up for air, she gasped and gently began to lie back, eager for him inside her, desperate and literally aching for his cock to thrust deep inside her, over and over again. Instead, he shifted her, gently but forcefully, face-down onto the mattress as she let out an involuntary moan of surprised bliss and guttural anticipation.

It was an unnatural, even unfamiliar sound, so spontaneous and primal she couldn't have controlled it, nor hidden it, had she tried. She recognized it as an animal noise devoid of grace or modesty, or even control. She wanted it this way. Wanted *him* this way—hard, fast, and in control.

This, Avery realized, was what she'd been waiting for. This, she suddenly knew, was what had been missing from their fantasies thus far. As independent and eager as she was to move mountains outside the bedroom, there were times, secret, desperate, even wanton times, when she wanted to be dominated, taken in a way she'd never been taken before, by a man she trusted enough to bring her to new heights as safely as he did energetically. Suddenly, face-down in the bedsheets and mouth gasping for air as he shifted her body into place, Avery felt his release of control and nearly came as a result.

The bed shifted beneath his weight as Branch knelt between her legs, spreading them shamelessly, all the while trilling his fingertips down her shoulder blades. Then he slithered alongside her back before playfully slapping and jiggling her upturned ass as mischievously as he did forcefully.

She gripped the fitted sheet beneath her, knuckles white, arms spread wide, mouth gasping for air as anticipation clutched her lungs with a furious grip unlike any she'd ever known before. The anticipation grew with each passing second, her senses on high alert, her body rigid and relaxed at the same time, her breath ragged even as he forced her to wait for his next move, as if knowing each passing moment only heightened her anticipation and thus, primed her for her next shuddering climax.

He was silent, mostly, save for the tender love pats he gave her jiggling bottom, growing warm and pink with his palms' attention as each rapturous slap and wiggle sent another spasm of pending release through her already vibrating core and straight down to her richly lathered mound, pressed tight and firm against the mattress as if it had been designed solely for that illicit purpose.

Her nipples, taut and stiff, rasped against the cotton sheet beneath her with each spank and wriggle, forcing her to silence pent-up screams by biting the nearest pillow, nearly severing it in half with the power of her clenched cries.

When he had thoroughly teased her into a face-down, ass-up, writhing tizzy, Branch gripped either side of her hips and tugged her gently upward to make room for his thighs, which gently propped her in a delightfully debased, prone position. She had always heard murmurs and hints about being *face-down, ass-up*, but had never known what the *fuss* was all about.

Until now, that was.

The pillow between her lips siphoned off her breath in a most delightful way, her nipples rubbing rapturously across the Egyptian cotton bedspread as Branch's left hand squeezed her left cheek while two of his long, splendid fingers whipped her eagerly throbbing pussy into a well-deserved froth.

Squeezing and fingering, rubbing and teasing, she was moments away from begging him to fuck her when she felt the first tentative slither of his fat, swollen tip against her aching clit. He knew just how firmly to press its thick and leaking tip against her mound, for just how long before she exploded in a pillow-biting climax that threatened to stop her heart completely.

And then, before she could recover from her first peak of the night, the length of his cock sliding gently deeper into her grateful pussy, ripe and yielding just for him, sent her spasming and climaxing anew. There was no pause this time, no thoughtful waiting out her tremors and hoarse, climactic squeals until teasing and tempting her into a fresh new wave of ecstatic release.

A hand on either side of her waist, gently lifting her another inch or two higher, Branch thrust deeper until his bony pelvis was pressed flat against the feminine curve of her arched backside. The motion, so unexpected and demonstrative, so manly and even domineering, sent her hurtling toward another massive climax as he remained wedged to the hilt and thrust deep inside her.

The swell of her orgasm constricted and stretched tight against his shaft, making them both shiver with delight. Still, he had come too often, and too recently, to join her in that first flurry of dizzying, intoxicating multiple orgasms so quickly.

Instead, he settled in, wedged tight and gripping her waist on either side, fingers so long and eager they practically circled her shuddering belly. Holding her in place, keeping her right where he wanted her, he began to gently thrust in and out, teasing her with the frenzied, piston-like pumping of an oil rig in overdrive.

Never less than gentle before, he seemed to sense her secret need for something . . . more. Something harder, more desperate, and masculine. He spoke not a word. He didn't have to. This time, his body, fiery and demanding, said everything his sensitive and boyish nature outside the bedroom couldn't. This time, for the first time, he took her in a way she'd never been taken before.

She lost herself, immune to the constraints of space and time. She quit counting her orgasms, her guttural screams, and unladylike curses as his nubile youth and enthusiasm pounded her with an energetic consistency that created an almost unbearable heat and friction where she desperately wanted it the most.

With every superhuman thrust and pulse, she slid farther into the abyss, tearing off the mattress cover, gripping it tightly between her clenched fists, mewling and muttering into the pillow she was surprised hadn't already burst into a flutter of damp, dewy feathers.

The headboard, so silent and chaste in the past, began to clatter and batter against the bedroom wall, drowned out only by Branch's animal grunting and her wild, raucous squeals.

Her nipples, once tender to the touch and grateful for the rasping sensation of flesh upon the bedsheet, grew raw and sensitive, rasping with each pinion thrust and throbbing quake. Her thighs ached in a most delightful way as he held her aloft, his grip so powerful her knees fairly hovered just above the squeaking mattress as his rhythm intensified and shuddering deep down to her very core, he exploded in a fiery release, filling her with his lust even as he wedged himself tight against her sweaty backside. At last he slid his fingers from around her waist, squeezing each cheek until they began to drag and drizzle her aching pussy along the last of his tumescence, as if knowing her aching clit was desperate for one last, desperate release.

Squeezing and dragging, slithering gently against her writhing bud, he did just that, giving her one last momentous explosion until he finally released her, the sound of his softly rigid prick sliding from deep within, barely covered by the gasping moans of her grateful release.

They literally collapsed in a heap of sore, untraceable limbs. His were hers, and hers were his, but half on top and hers above and heaving, sweaty and slightly embarrassed, she turned and clung to him with an almost desperate combination of need and gratitude.

She wept quietly against his throat, silently hoping he would mistake the surprising show of emotion for yet another massive aftershock of desire. If he did, Branch was gentleman enough not to comment on the flood of emotions, during *or* after.

He might have just deflowered her like a virgin on prom night, but instantly his sensitive nature returned, and he held her closely, quietly, until she drifted into a pure, unadulterated state of sheer exhaustion.

Chapter Twenty-four: Branch

"Merry Christmas Eve," Branch whispered, gently shutting the bedroom door even as Avery's snores, as lusty and unfiltered as her moans only a few hours before, drifted through the thin, fabricated wood between them.

He tiptoed away, shoes in one hand, clothes in the other, changing quickly in the guest bathroom before raiding her fridge for the most appetizing thing in sight, a tall, brown can of iced mocha from a smattering of other canned and bottled beverages on colorful display atop the bottom shelf.

He shut the door quietly and opened the can to a modicum of hiss and spray, rushing it to his mouth and savoring the bittersweet java and cream combination until the can was half-empty and he sank back against the kitchen counter, eyes rolling back in his head like a slot machine hitting the jackpot with sheer, caffeinated bliss.

He hadn't tasted anything that good since, well . . . since Avery's musky lust on the tip of his tongue, only a few days before in that very kitchen. He smirked at the memory, hardly believing his good luck even as his limbs still felt the pleasant soreness of a good and proper fuck fest that still made his belly tremor and his cheeks blush at the sudden recollection.

Branch was no hesitant virgin, far from it. Life had been good to him after high school. A gym membership and some contact lenses helped him leave behind the thick glasses and scrawny gawkiness of his high school days, helping him ease into manhood one blind date, booty call, dating app, and chance encounter at a time.

But always, the ghost of Avery Balthazar lingered in the back of his mind. Despite the half-dozen words they might have said to each other back in high school, despite a head full of unrealized fantasies he'd constructed around her, in and out of the rain, Branch couldn't shake the thought, the very real thought, that Avery was, well . . . the one who got away.

It had soured and tainted every so-called relationship he'd had after graduation, gently, subconsciously, but inevitably driving away every girl he ever bedded until, eventually, he just . . . gave up. Threw himself into his work with the same passion and eagerness he'd always spent fantasizing about smart, sexy, aloof, and unavailable Avery.

Eventually, he'd given up on ever seeing her again. That was, until she'd literally strutted back into his life a mere forty-eight hours ago. That meant he had one day left before she gave her ill-fated pitch and he was forced to reject her. No doubt she'd turn tail and run back to Daddy, literally, jetting back to Manhattan while cursing his name the whole way there.

Sadly, it was a necessary evil. As much affection as he'd already had for Avery, and despite growing even closer to her over the last few days, there was simply no way he was going to give up everything he'd built, brick by brick, so that her stepfather could fold it into his massive corporation and turn all his golden ideas into platinum profits for his own sake. It had been a fool's mission from the get-go, but one he was glad Avery had made herself, despite how it was doomed to inevitably end.

Then again, he still had twenty-four hours left to change her mind. A whole day to remind her who she was, where she'd come from, and how great it might be if she could join him and expand the world he'd built, one, eh, fantasy at a time. And with the few hours he had left before she inevitably woke up, he intended to do just that.

Without glancing at the time, he hit the first number in his contact list, gently shutting Avery's front door behind him. He was already on his bike, pedaling quickly down her cobblestone drive street when a groggy, irritable voice answered.

"Yeah?"

Branch chuckled merrily, noting the many-colored lights and flashing reindeer and snowman displays on every yard but Avery's as he pedaled fiercely down her street. "Now, is that any way to wish your boss a Merry Christmas Eve?"

"Branch, what the actual, bro?"

A second voice on the other end of the line murmured something dark and deep and guttural from nearby. Spike grunted playfully, "It's just the old man giving us a crank call. Go back to sleep."

Branch smirked. Turned out he wasn't the only one in town getting a little late-night holiday nookie these days. "Tell Jevon I'm sorry, but going back to sleep is *not* an option. I'm gonna need him, too."

Spike was suddenly chuckling nervously, stammering as if their relationship was some big secret. "That . . . that's not Jevon, silly."

"Sure it is, bud. I'd recognize that sarcastic tone and baritone voice anywhere."

There was a playful giggle, a rustling of the sheets, and then a surprisingly giddy Spike murmuring, just out of earshot, "Stop, Jevon. Time to get up now."

Branch made a face but couldn't afford to be a prude now, not with a lapful of spunk drying on his belly even as he pedaled. "I thought we were off for the holidays," Spike reminded him, sounding more and more energized with each passing moment. "Remember your big announcement at the warehouse yesterday?"

"You were off the rest of the week, Spike, old buddy, old pal, but . . . change of plans."

"What if I already *had* plans?" Spike spoke with the lazy gusto of someone who didn't really want another outcome but who just wanted to argue before the inevitability of his situation came to bear.

Branch spoke with the assured resolve of someone who signed the paychecks—the very generous paychecks, that was—every week. "Well, you can put them on hold and spend a few grand more on whatever it was you had scheduled, because this change of plans comes with a massive bonus."

Spike's reply was blunt, somber, and immediate. "I'm in. Definitely. Count me in. Let's go!"

From the depths of the speaker phone, Jevon's voice chimed in as well, "Me, too, boss! All in!"

Branch chuckled and pedaled leisurely, dictating a variety of to-do items, menus, measurables, and deliverables as he steered idly about the town and promising to follow-up with the dynamic duo in a few hours.

"You know it's five in the AM, right boss?" Spike murmured as, in the background, coffee sputtered in a machine and mugs and spoons clattered with aching familiarity. "On . . . Christmas Eve?"

Branch eased effortlessly back into boss mode. "And? If the grocery stores aren't open yet, just grab what you can at a convenience store. The rest of the places should have websites, right? Try to order online and . . . what? What's so funny?"

"Nothing, just . . . I haven't seen you this excited in a while, boss. This wouldn't have anything to do with Avery coming back into town now, would it?"

"Of course it doesn't," Branch snapped unconvincingly. On the other end, giggles aplenty greeted his obvious denial. "Fine, whatever, anyway, you two get your asses in gear, and I'll see you at the warehouse in a few hours. And Spike? Jevon?"

"Yeah, boss?" Their voices merged, a combination of deep and high and everything in between.

"Merry Christmas Eve, guys. Let's make it a year to remember, okay?"

"It already is," Spike murmured, clattering coffee mugs in the background.

"Yeah," Jevon concurred. "I can't remember anyone ever waking my ass up this early before!"

They were both still giggling when Branch ended the call, sliding his phone into the basket clasped to his handlebars as he lazily pedaled through his quiet, lakeside town.

The air was cool but not quite crisp, a perfect fit for his admittedly wrinkled button-down collar shirt and trademark khaki pants. It soothed his feverish skin, still blisteringly hot and intermittently blushing from his late-night lust fest with Avery.

He marveled, as he pedaled, at how quickly one's world could tilt, tumble and slip upside-down. Two days ago, he'd been as eager and content as ever, breaking ground on one new project even as he put the finishing touches on several more. Solidifying marketing language and graphics, eagerly engaging with his dozen or so employees on the daily as he went through his routine happily.

Or so he thought.

And then, literally out of nowhere, Avery had sauntered into his office and . . . instant upheaval. Every long, limber, dramatically beautiful inch of her harkened back to his not-so-distant past, making him realize he hadn't buried her as deeply as he'd thought in his confused subconscious.

Old feelings sprang to life, merging with new emotions, confusion, apprehension, and finally, anticipation. To learn that she'd fantasized about him back in school, as eagerly as he had her, had been a revelation in a day of revelations—and Branch hadn't looked back.

How could he have? Between flirting, fighting, fidgeting, and fucking, there hadn't been a minute's peace! And now, on her final day in town, he found himself as addicted to Avery as he was to the rush and grind of building his arts and entertainment empire. What's more, he was as invested in keeping her around as she was in whisking him away.

As peaceful as the town of Lakemont looked to him at that very moment, beneath the surface, his mind whirled with the possibilities, the angles, the opportunities that existed if he could just sway the tide and convince her what was so special about the town she couldn't wait to leave a few short years ago.

He smirked proudly, passing the restaurants, the cafes, the diners, and the drive-thrus he'd crafted from the ground up, virtually out of thin air, all of them paling in comparison to his latest challenge.

The challenge, he realized, of his life.

It was daunting, it was downright scary, but Branch was nothing if not resourceful. He knew, deep down in his gut, that Avery was at a tipping point in her life. She was so strong and confident, so independent and capable, and yet, there was a part of her that *wanted* to be convinced. The same way she'd wanted to be taken the night before, Branch knew she could be steered into altering the course of her life — if only he could get her to listen.

Branch smiled at the prospect, finding himself racing faster and faster toward the warehouse with a combination of apprehension and anticipation. She had come to town to pitch him the offer of a lifetime, and in the end, Branch would wind up pitching her instead.

He thought Avery had been exaggerating when she'd told him that failure was not an option, but now he knew exactly what she'd meant. The only difference was that back then, she'd been talking about business.

Suddenly, irrevocably, Branch knew that to fail today would mean giving up on the chance, the romance, of a lifetime. He had let her walk out of his life once before, but not again. Not this time.

This was, quite literally, the deal of a lifetime. And like Avery before him, Branch was no longer willing to fail.

CHAPTER TWENTY-FIVE: AVERY

"Branch?"

Avery was just wriggling into her casual gray crinkle skirt when she heard the telltale beep-bloop of the front door code being keyed in from outside. Like a schoolgirl giddy in the throes of her first taste of insatiable puppy love, she raced across the living room floor amidst the pounding of her heart and clattering of her sensible black ballet flats.

"You're conducting business meetings in your home now?" Her father's voice, rich and baritone, boomed through the rafters as he stood just inside the open doorway, offering her a curiously knowing smile.

"Dad?" Her shock was so severe he must have read it on her face.

She was only grateful she'd dressed for another day of work and play at the warehouse and not their first unhinged tryst of the morning, as she'd been tempted to do. God only knew what her stepfather might have thought if he'd found her standing in the middle of the living room in a slinky sheer negligee—and not much else.

"Not at all. I just . . . why didn't you call first?"

"Do I have to?" Her stepfather chuckled in an uncharacteristically breezy way. His cane in one hand, he held a slim package under the other arm.

"No, of course not. I just . . . you haven't been shy about calling all weekend."

He gave her a wry grin and waved his cane at the cozy new interior of the old homestead. "Well, that clearly wasn't getting any results, so I decided to stop in to say . . . Merry Christmas Eve!"

She brightened, hoping he might not notice the undergarments scattered hither and yon about the kitchen and living room, the empty bottles of champagne and half-empty glasses that were, so far, her only nod at the holiday festivities the rest of the town was currently engaged in. Of all her deepest, darkest fantasies she'd decided to indulge in that weekend, cleaning up after herself clearly hadn't been one.

"And to you."

He stood awkwardly, sliding the sedately wrapped gift atop the kitchen counter as they lingered in the foyer. The wrapping paper was a subdued forest green, and the bow a richly sumptuous maroon velvet.

"Something to drink?" she asked, just as awkwardly. Her heart was still pounding at the sudden intrusion, her father's presence like a bucket of cold water on the feverish pace and lusty, uh . . . activities of the last two days.

"Obviously," he murmured with a wave of his cane as she busied herself with the crystal decanter set atop the rough-hewn brass bar cart just outside the cozy kitchen nook.

"Why are you really here, Dad?" she asked, handing him a rocks glass half full of bourbon.

He sipped it greedily, easing onto one of the rattan barstools that accented the eclectic boho furnishings she'd had no part in choosing and yet, somehow, had grown to favor over the brief holiday weekend.

"Can't a father wish his own daughter happy holidays without getting the third-degree in the process?" His rich, baritone voice made Avery feel like she'd suddenly been transported back to their corporate headquarters in Manhattan.

She smirked, the decanter still in hand, hovering over her own glass until she decided *screw it* and poured herself a healthy dollop. It was Christmas Eve, after all. She'd indulged in every other conceivable decadence this holiday season. Why not with a mid-morning belt of twenty-year-old Kentucky bourbon as well?

She took a long, burning sip before fixing Archibald with a curious, knowing gaze across the bar top. "A normal father, yes. You? Not without an ulterior motive."

He chuckled dryly as he set his heavy rocks glass down on the counter with a resounding clatter. She inched closer, peering down the hallway at the long glass panes on either side of the red-painted door. "Are there more bags outside, or . . ."

He got the hint. "Oh, I can't stay, dear. I just popped in for a quick progress report and . . ." He tapped the top of the present, careful not to ruffle the carefully tied bow on top. "To give you your gift, of course."

She sank onto the armrest of the couch across from him, crossing her legs primly as if to distance herself from the strong sizzle of sex that still hung in the air.

"Are we . . . exchanging gifts now?"

Other than tuition and living expenses, of course, Avery couldn't remember the last time her father gave her an actual gift. A present one could hold and turn over and unwrap and discover. A . . . surprise. And even those monetary expenditures, they both knew, were an investment in her education so that she could one day secede him at Balthazar Broadcasting.

He glanced slightly down at her from atop his swivel barstool. "Of a sort." Then he slapped the knees of his tailored gray linen slacks in a vague sign of growing impatience. "So, any progress on your very own *Mission Impossible,* yet?"

She girded her loins and sipped slowly from the rocks glass, the piquant sting of alcohol only adding to the surreal nature of her father's visit and the fact that, only hours earlier, she'd been making animal noises while screaming face-first into a pillow, Branch Asher wedged deep inside her. She squirmed again and struggled not to blush anew. "I still have twenty-four hours to seal the deal, remember, Pops?"

He shrugged, surprisingly casual as opposed to his iron fist the other day back in the corporate boardroom. Avery, on the other hand, hadn't been so tense since he'd introduced her high atop their corporate headquarters two days hence. "A father can hope, can't he?"

Avery ran her hand along the armrest beneath her, realizing with a sudden blush that it was probably the only piece of furniture in the house she and Branch hadn't consummated.

Yet.

"We're making . . . progress," she said, tongue firmly planted in her cheek.

Her father squinted at something on the countertop and with the brass eagle tip of his hand-carved cane, hooked a corner of a discarded pair of wadded-up boxer briefs that were, even at a casual glance, clearly not her own.

"I can see that, dear."

"Geez, sorry about that," she bluffed with her heart pounding and blush sizzling her cheeks as she leaned forward to pluck the offending undergarment from the eagle's beak. "I've been so busy chatting up Branch about joining Balthazar Broadcasting that I've been living like a sorority girl again." She shoved the offending undergarments, still damp, she noted ickily, beneath a colorful boho throw pillow at her side.

"More like a frat *boy*," he remarked, lifting the snifter to his lips and sipping gently. "But I'm glad to see you're . . . keeping busy."

For the first time, she wondered if her father had included hidden cameras during the house's miraculous overhaul while she'd been busy matriculating at University. The thought literally made her blanch, even more so than the lust-soaked boxer briefs under the pillow at her side.

"Never been busier," she said with a wry nod, realizing

that everything she said was sounding dirty. Perhaps she really was devolving back into a sorority sister on this unexpected holiday weekend of sudden debauchery.

So why was she enjoying it so damn much?

Her father sipped his bourbon and glanced around the room. She cocked her head subtly. "Is that . . . it?"

He seemed surprised by the question. "I believe so. Why?"

She was just as surprised by his reply. "You mean . . . you're not going to pester me about Branch anymore?"

"Did I ever?"

"Only every moment since you made me the head of the Themed Eateries and Entertainment department."

He gave her a curious stare, the silence in the room growing subtly ominous as she waited for whatever proclamation he'd clearly flown across the country to make. "Yes, well, on second thought . . . I *may* have been mistaken in sending you on this little reconnaissance mission, Avery."

Avery stiffened. His face hadn't changed, but his tone certainly had. From curiosity to disappointment, she had never felt so . . . dismissed. This after a lifetime of casual dismissal.

"I wouldn't necessarily agree."

"You don't have to, of course. I created the division. I can dissolve it if need be."

"Dissolve it? Whatever for?"

He shrugged, seeming wistful as he glanced at the various changes and upgrades his property management team had made around the old house. "You will understand when you're in charge one day, dear. Sometimes things look very different on paper than they do in real life."

"Such as?"

He sighed, not quite wearily, but heavily just the same. "Such as . . . this place. This town. This idea of mine that Branch would be an easy mark."

"This all sounds very curious coming from you,

Archibald."

His smile was as wry as it was weary. "Does it, dear?"

"Of course it does. You never miss a mark. You always get everything you want."

"Not everything, dear." His smile was surprisingly . . . gentle. So surprisingly calm, she was immediately distrustful. She wondered if that said more about her stepfather than it did about her.

"Oh yeah, old man? Like what?"

"Like your mother, for instance."

She stiffened. They rarely spoke about her mother, his ex-wife, or the fractured relationship that resulted in the not surprisingly acrimonious divorce. "I think you made it clear when you slept with your new assistant that you weren't interested in keeping Mom around anymore. Or me, for that matter."

He was, as ever, unphased by anything as insignificant as mere facts. "Your mother had moved back here long before I . . . strayed, Avery. We both know that."

"Only because you kept her isolated in that penthouse apartment, Dad. She had no friends, no social life, no contacts, and, well . . . no you. You took her coming back here as abandonment when it was simply a natural reaction to being displaced. She explained all this to you. I heard her. I heard you dismissing her, so to say you *couldn't have her* is a bit of a rewriting of history, Dad."

He peered back at her after staring at his lap for the length of her sudden and unexpectedly passionate discourse. He held up a single hand, quieting them both. "I didn't come here to stir up old memories, dear. I only came to say that plans don't always come to fruition, that our lives are not always what they seem to be and that, in the end, we have to be in charge of our own destinies."

She smirked, finding her glass dry and her throat, or at

least her confused brain, hungry for another shot of courage. Still, something about her father's confessional tone and vaguely regretful poise stilled her from standing and crossing the room to top off both their glasses.

"Are you . . . okay, Dad?"

He nodded, chin up and eyes returning to their formerly steely gaze. "Of course, dear. I just . . . wasn't prepared for how this house might make me feel. It's been . . ."

"Years," she finished for him. "I know, Dad. Trust me, I know. I . . . it's part of why I've been a little lost myself this weekend. But I've still got today, right? To get back on track and seal this deal, once and for all?"

He chuckled wryly, standing beside his barstool as she rose as well. He tapped the present with his free hand, leaning on his cane with the other. "Don't forget your present, dear."

She cocked her head, just shy of reaching out for it. "Don't you want me to open it now?"

He shook his head, already walking away. "Oh, no, I'd be embarrassed. Besides, it's a Christmas present, dear. At least wait until midnight, okay?"

"If you insist."

They stood in the doorway, a sleek limousine idling at the curb. *Wow,* she marveled. *He really hadn't been planning on staying long.* He lingered atop the welcome mat, as crisp and new and generically attractive as everything else about the rehabbed house. She had so many questions, and despite the stretch limousine purring smoothly at the curb, her stepfather suddenly seemed in no hurry to leave.

"So, you really flew all the way here just to get an update?"

He shrugged casually, an evasive look in his eye. "Well, it was on my way to the Malibu compound, obviously, so . . . why not?"

She smirked knowingly. "And here I thought you flew all the way to California to see little old me."

He nodded somberly, eyes showing no sign of deceit. "I did, actually. The trip to Malibu was an afterthought. Been awhile since I've spent Christmas on the beach."

"Won't you be lonely, Dad?"

He gave her a casually leering wink. "Who says I'll be alone, dear?"

Her face fell dramatically. "Gross."

He made a casual *yes, I'm an old lecher, and no, I'm never going to change* shrug, and as if by happenstance, their eyes met one last time. He nodded at a lantern hanging fashionably from the overhang just above the doorway. "Do you like the upgrades I made to the old place?"

She nodded. "Very much so. But I'm more surprised you kept it in the first place."

He patted the doorway. "It has a certain sentimental value, I suppose." Then he paused, giving her one last penetrating gaze. "Like I said, I wasn't prepared for just how I'd feel standing here again. I imagine, well . . . I imagine this must feel even more like a homecoming for you, Avery."

"I'm not gonna lie, Pops. It's dredged up old feelings I thought I'd buried long ago."

His voice grew grave, even as he struggled to keep a stiff upper lip. "Yes, well, the past has a way of catching up to you. I thought I could avoid it, dear. I thought I could keep both of us protected from that part of our lives, but this assignment, this task, has brought us right back to ground, hasn't it?"

"You can say that again."

He winked, holding his cane aloft as if signaling his imminent departure. "No, dear, I think . . . I think for once, I've said more than enough."

She smirked. "Don't tell me you're getting sentimental in your old age, Pops?"

"I suppose it's inevitable. Believe it or not, your mother and I shared some good times here. I didn't want to discard that entirely."

"Even if you swore that you'd never come back to Lake-mont?"

"And yet . . . here I am."

"I wish you'd stay a little longer, Dad." Surprisingly, for once, Avery meant it. She'd never seen her father this way before, so open and exposed, and dare she admit it, vulnerable. Obviously, he didn't feel comfortable lingering in those emotions long either, hence the car literally running at the curb.

He seemed to sense the bittersweet resignation in her voice. Or, perhaps, the naked vulnerability in his own. Either way, he stiffened yet again. "Duty calls, dear, but we'll have all the time in the world to . . . chat . . . once you get back to Manhattan, right?"

Suddenly for once, the prospect sounded supremely unappealing. Not talking to her father, per se, but the thought of leaving little Lakemont and all its various . . . charms. She sighed and stiffened in the doorway, hedging her bets with a suddenly cautious reply. "Sure, Dad. After Christmas, then?"

He waved his cane in farewell and turned, surprisingly deftly. She watched him hobble down the lane, the driver emerging from the limousine and opening the back door with a curt, efficient nod.

In moments the car was driving away, leaving her standing in the doorway wondering what to do with the rest of the day. To say nothing of, well . . . the rest of her life.

No doubt her father had meant the impromptu visit as a last-minute pep talk, a Hail Mary pass to get her to gird her loins and gear up for that day's pitch. Instead, it had quite the opposite effect. Seeing her father again had reminded her of the grim duties that awaited her back *home* in the big city. And yet, standing in that doorway, revitalized but not removed, she had never felt more at home in her life.

She idly wondered if her father hadn't realized that as well.

If he hadn't swooped in on his way to Malibu that morning to remind her of her true home and that ultimately it was her choice to make where she wound up. To fail would mean she would lose her place atop the gleaming, corporate Ivory Tower in Manhattan, but suddenly she wasn't convinced that was such a bad thing after all.

Suddenly, in fact, she was learning to redefine the very idea of failure itself. And she wondered, turning in the doorway to face the day in earnest, if that wasn't the gift her father had just given her after all.

Chapter Twenty-six: Branch

"No, to the left a little."

Branch stood on the landing at the top of the spiral staircase overlooking the warehouse floor, adjusting the last of the stockings while Jevon and Spike glanced upward at his progress.

They . . . were less than impressed.

"My left or your left?"

Spike sighed, pointing. "That left."

Branch shot him daggers. "So my right then?"

Spike rolled his eyes. "We're talking semantics here, but sure, yes, fine, just . . . right there!"

Branch hung the stocking, then stood, arching his back before glancing down at the demanding duo, resplendent in matching ugly Christmas sweaters and knitted Santa caps, looking every bit as if they were off to host some downtown Christmas parade.

The three of them had been at it for hours, the boys patiently guiding Branch this way and that as he created a temporary winter wonderland that he hoped would make for a welcome surprise once Avery showed up.

That was, if she ever did.

They were supposed to meet that afternoon for her *big pitch presentation*, but he had other plans in mind and wanted to set the scene the best he could on short notice. And if he was honest, to soften the blow when he inevitably turned her down flat.

"How's it look?"

Jevon frowned. "It would help if you turned on the lights."

"Oh, shit! Right . . ." Branch reached for the universal switch on his end of the extension cord connected to the miles of Christmas lights wound around the loft railing that ran for one entire stretch of the warehouse wall. After he flicked it on, the entire loft blinked to life with winking colored and white lights.

He didn't have to hear their approval. He saw it in the soft, warm, appreciative glow of their joint smiles.

"Nice!" they murmured in unison, shoulder to shoulder as they peered up at him, eyes dewy and moist like some old married couple watching their kids' first recital.

Branch was doubtful. He had a feeling they were just shining him on in order to be done with the whole process and start their vacation officially. "Yeah? You sure?"

Spike rolled his eyes. "Yes, we're sure. Now . . . can we go?"

Jevon nodded. "I mean, it's our Christmas Eve, too, right?"

Branch began the slow, methodical descent down the wrought iron stairs, admiring the hanging stockings and winking bulbs he passed along the way. "Oh, I'm sorry. I would have thought going home with fat bonuses in your stockings would have made up for the few hours we've spent in each other's company this fine holiday afternoon."

"Few hours?" Spike's face was radiant — and indignant.

"Try, like, six hours." Jevon groaned for emphasis.

Branch had reached the bottom of the stairs and was rattling around in the ice bowl atop the break room countertop for a bottle of champagne. "It was four hours, Jevon," he said as he popped the bottle with a flourish. "And I tacked on a little extra to your bonus checks for your trouble, so . . . you're welcome."

Spike inched closer, licking his lips greedily. "Is that . . . for us?"

"Of course," Branch chuckled, topping off three plastic champagne flutes evenly. "A little shift drink after all your hard work today."

The two gave each other an excited high-five before reaching for their cups.

"A toast, first!" Branch reminded them playfully before they could sip.

"God. Fine. Yes." Jevon chuckled with the exasperated sigh of an old man waiting for his granddaughter to tie her shoes for the sixth time before heading out to the park where, truth be told, he didn't really want to go in the first place.

"To new beginnings," Branch said, hoisting his glass toward the suddenly confused couple.

"What? New? Beginning?" Spike asked dramatically, dragging the emo flop of rich black hair away from his eyes as if to see better. "Wait, is this about the new drive-in?"

Jevon narrowed a thick eyebrow. "Or have you got something else in mind?"

Branch couldn't have been more amused by their suspicious minds. "Guys, it's almost New Year's Eve. Can't I just toast to new beginnings . . . in general?"

The two gave each other a knowing look before Spike murmured, "Not the way you've been acting this weekend, boss."

"Yeah," Jevon chimed in. "Methinks your new beginning has more than just a little to do with that smokin' hot MILF from the other day."

"She's not a mother," Branch said, too quickly.

Jevon and Spike gave each other a knowing look. "So it is about her then? New beginnings as in . . . what, exactly?"

Their playfully sing-song voices blended into one harmonious roast, like the red and green cacophony of their ugly Christmas sweaters. "Like, are you going to propose?"

"Was it love at first sight?"

"Do you think she'll like living in the loft?"

"You can totally leave the lights on all year if it helps set the mood, boss man."

"Well, I mean, the white ones anyway . . ."

Branch was used to their nonstop trolling, but the bubbly and the promise of one last night with Avery had him in a vaguely confessional mood.

He might have found it sad that Spike and Jevon were about as close as he had to actual friends—if they weren't such good company. He liked spending time with them, and their complaints notwithstanding, the boys usually liked spending time with him.

And he was just fine with that. "Boys, we just met."

Spike waved his champagne flute accusingly. "I call BS on that! You said you two went to school together."

Branch groaned and topped off their glasses. He'd been nervous all day. About endings, about beginnings, about that day, and in particular, that night. "Must you two remember everything I say?"

"Hey, you hired us because we pay attention to details, remember?"

"Yeah, to contracts and signage, not . . . personal stuff."

Spike and Jevon shared a conspiratorial look that bordered suspiciously on pity. "Well, it's been a while since you've had any real personal stuff to pay attention to," Jevon noted as Spike nodded approvingly.

Branch sank onto a barstool at the Plexiglas breakroom counter. "Fair enough, I just . . . we've all been busy, right?"

Spike nudged Jevon's hip playfully. "You're never too busy for love, right, boo?"

Jevon winked saucily. "The busier, the better."

Branch was less than impressed. "Gross. Listen, the day I take love advice from actual fetuses, I'm trading in my man card, okay?"

The boys took it as a challenge, if not quite a compliment.

"Still, we're not wrong, are we?"

"No, you're not. It's just . . . complicated."

Spike seemed downright indignant. "What's complicated? You like her, she likes you . . . make it work."

Jevon joined in enthusiastically, glancing at the champagne bottle as if to guess its vintage. "Yeah, dude, you built a whole entertainment eatery empire out of a coffee shop covered in monster movie posters. How hard can love be?"

Branch wished he had the kind of confidence in himself that his employees did in him. "That might have worked back in high school, guys, but . . . we've got responsibilities now. Jobs. Careers. Goals."

The boys shared another knowing wink.

"Stop doing that," Branch chided them playfully.

"Doing what?" Spike giggled. Clearly, the bubbly was getting to him.

"Doing that whole wink-wink, nudge-nudge thing like you're sharing a joke I'm not in on."

Jevon's voice grew as serious as it ever got. "The only joke, boss, is that you can't see what's right in front of your own eyes."

"Such as?"

Jevon set his glass down, if only to wave his arms dramatically as his sage, twenty-something wisdom began to spew forth like water from a sprinkler head. "You wanna know the last time you decorated for Christmas, boss? Never. You wanna know the last time you catered a lunch at the ass crack of dawn for some hot chick on Christmas Eve? Never. You wanna know the last time you gave us the holidays off? Never. You wanna know the last time you came to work wearing the same clothes two days in a row, wrinkled as hell, and clearly picked up off said hot chick's floor? Uh, never. So . . . clearly, something's up, and if you're too blind to see it, then you're simply beyond our expert help."

"Not something," Spike reminded his cheeky young lover with a playful hip check. "Some *one*."

"Not just someone," Jevon chimed in playfully, both of them clearly enjoying themselves. "Avery."

Branch's very body jolted at the sound of her name. As if piling it on, the boys mimicked kissing motions and noises as Branch rolled his eyes, finding it hard not to feel seen despite their limited life — and love — experience. Then again, they did seem pretty happy together so . . . maybe they were on to something after all.

Spike waved his half-empty champagne flute. "So . . . what new beginnings, actually?"

Jevon nodded, as if expecting an answer.

Branch sighed heavily, wishing he had one. The fact was, he had no idea what was going to happen that night. Or the next day, or the day after that. He realized it had been a long time since he could make that statement.

It felt better than he cared to admit.

"I guess we'll see after tonight, huh, kids?" Branch stood, butterflies still dancing in his belly despite the crisp, dry bubbly and the promise of Avery's imminent — he hoped — arrival.

The boys exchanged one last knowing wink. "I guess that's our cue to go, huh, boss?"

"I mean, you don't have to go home, guys, but . . ."

"We can't stay here. Gotcha, gotcha . . ."

There were hugs and murmurs, chuckles and teasing on the way to the warehouse door. Jevon and Spike breezed through as one, colorful sweaters and Christmas socks aglow in the late afternoon light. Branch stood alone in the empty parking lot, watching as the boys tumbled onto the blacktop, making much of putting on their Mohawk helmets before boarding their matching blue and pink scooters with their usual combination of energy and aplomb and touchy-feely, good-natured flirting.

Branch felt a sudden pang of regret, or perhaps even envy, watching Spike and Jevon help each other with the clasps and the buttons of their helmets, each waiting for the other to start his engine before glancing back at Branch for one last good-bye.

He could only imagine what he must have looked like to them, standing alone in the parking lot in his sad, wrinkled clothes, waiting for them to leave together, his future as uncertain as it had ever been. What a sad sack he must have seemed, and yet he felt, strange as it seemed, rather content. It might have been a temporary feeling.

After all, Avery could be on a jet back to Manhattan that very night if things didn't go as planned. Then again, she might not, and the fact that he had even the least bit of a fighting chance was giving him life in a way he hadn't felt in, well . . . since the last time she left him standing there, waving, the same way he was right now.

He blinked himself back to life, standing idly in the late afternoon California sky over his little hometown. The boys were still in the process of leaving. The motors still purred, their hybrid scooters part of the employee benefits plan, and as such, complimentary to everyone who worked at the warehouse. That was, after they passed their 90-day probationary period, naturally. He waved some more. They waved some more, still lingering atop the putt-putting scooters until it grew too awkward to remain that way any longer.

A few more waves and they drifted from the parking lot, turning left onto the main drag that would take them back into town. Branch lingered just a little longer, enjoying the afternoon sun on his face and feeling more alone than ever.

He shouldn't have. He was used to being alone, after all. Used to working holidays and not decorating, burning the midnight oil with a dedicated team of like-minded young folk who, he thought, never worried, cared, or noticed that Christmas was just another day.

Suddenly, Branch realized that it *was* a special day. And one he wanted to share with the most special person he knew. Perhaps, he thought wistfully, Christmas was only special if he had a person to share it with. As he waited for her, he wondered how he could ever go back to not caring about her again. How life could ever go back once she inevitably boarded that *Learjet* back to New York and left him stranded in Lakemont all over again.

And what he might finally do to change her mind, once and for all . . .

Chapter Twenty-seven: Avery

"Happy holidays . . ."

Avery cruised through town, a vaguely cheery Christmas playlist oozing merrily from the cell phone gently nestled inside the basket on her bike as she pedaled north in no particular hurry.

"Happy holidays . . ."

She found herself singing along with a wistful Peggy Lee, a cheeky grin on her face as her belly tightened with every rotation of her pedals, knowing full well that they would inevitably bring her back to him.

To Branch. The man who'd brought her to orgasm more times in one weekend than, well, let's face it, all the men in her previous sex life, such as it was, combined. And that was just that morning.

It wasn't just the nonstop, drop-dead, sinful sex, Avery admitted, if only to herself. He'd been thoughtful, kind, generous, considerate, playful, funny, smart, wise, and in his own way, inspirational.

As she wove through town, drifting closer to the warehouse with every turn of her pedals, Avery tried to keep track of Branch's numerous themed eateries. From the one that started it all, the *Creature Café* in the refurbished strip mall on the edge of town, past the desserts-only food truck field, *Calorie Park*, on past the *Sweet Spot*, a candy store that sold only toy-based snacks. Each one was bustling with activity and more colorful, fun, and successful than the last.

Avery found it almost hard to imagine the quiet, shy,

unassuming — if totally hunky — Branch Asher she knew from school had it in him. And yet, his creativity, imagination, and success rivaled nearly any of the organizations that Balthazar Broadcasting had recruited into their umbrella corporation over the years, and that included television stations, movie studios, record companies, and famous podcasters.

As she pedaled through her quiet hometown, even more quiet on this placidly beautiful holiday afternoon, she felt the vague sting of envy whenever she passed another Branch milestone, be it a retro malt shop or vibing juke joint. He had done so much with the six years they'd been apart, and all Avery had done was bide her time until she had the MBA that was mandatory for working at her father's company.

And for what? Just to fly all the way across the country on her first assignment and try to buy Avery out with an offer that was far below his own potential net worth? She felt conflicted, torn between her family responsibility and her new-found affection and goodwill for Branch.

Perhaps that was why, when the warehouse appeared, funky and hip with its colorfully graffitied walls and old-fashioned, movie theater marquee-style lettering overhead, she . . . just kept pedaling.

Not because she wasn't dying to see Branch again. She was, God knew she was. Her entire body ached to see him again, to touch and smell and taste the whole of him. To hear his laugh and warm to his smile and simmer in the affection of his cheerful, penetrating gaze.

Avery supposed she just wanted one last loop around *Vintage Village*, home of Branch and Company's latest half-dozen popular themed eateries, and beyond, to the vacant acre or two of recently cleared land bearing the new construction sign that read, *Coming Soon, Another New Adventure from Asher Enterprises*.

She felt a different type of excitement, reading that sign —

pride. Proud to know the man behind it and what he now meant to her. She smiled, no longer envious or anxious or nervous or apprehensive, only . . . excited . . . as she turned before the pavement ended at the new work site and pedaled back, more quickly than before, toward the warehouse just around the corner.

The morning had turned to mid-morning and eventually, afternoon. The sun warmed her skin much as the old-timey Christmas carols warmed her heart. It had been years since she'd listened to Christmas music, a tradition only her mother kept going, and after her, they had always made her sad.

But this unexpected homecoming had been healing in more ways than one. Rather than find her mourning her mother even more, it had found Avery celebrating her more than ever. Her independence, her bravery, the sheer audacity of divorcing one of the richest men in the world only to return to her hometown and, thankfully, dragging her daughter along for the ride.

How different Avery's life might have been if she'd stayed behind with her stepfather in Manhattan, as he'd desperately wanted her to at the time. And tempting as it had been to a teenage girl whose life had just been turned upside-down, the city lights, staggeringly large penthouse apartment, bustling streets, endless fashion, parties, and nonstop noise, Avery somehow knew her place was back in Lakemont, by her mother's side.

While her mother was too busy fighting tooth and nail for half of her ex-husband's fortune—which was, obviously, challenging, considering there was no prenuptial agreement—Avery had found solace in the normalcy, the familiarity, of high school.

It was her routine every day, her excuse not to go back to New York and fall under her stepfather's spell. And of course, her chance to gaze at Branch and fantasize about what a normal life with a normal guy might feel like.

Never in a million years, after finally accepting her stepfather's offer of college and a career and leaving on the day of graduation to begin life anew in the ivy league, could Avery have imagined how sentimental, warm, and downright sexy her eventual homecoming might have been.

And now that it was nearly at an end, Avery was more determined than ever not to waste a single minute of it . . .

CHAPTER TWENTY-EIGHT: BRANCH

"Avery?"

Branch heard the warehouse door open, shivering with a combination of dread and anticipation as her voice chirped out in reply, "Branch? The hell?"

He snorted at her comically frustrated agitation, suddenly remembering in all his planning that day that he'd forgotten that she didn't quite know her way around the warehouse.

Yet.

He stood abruptly from his warm, familiar barstool to enter the openness of the warehouse entryway just past the breakroom area. "Shit, sorry . . . coming!" His body fairly trembled to hear her. He had thought, in his subtly simmering paranoia, that she might not show after all. That all his hard work, all his worrying and fretting, planning and dreaming and even decorating, had all been for naught.

There was a slight tremor to her voice as well. He hoped it might be anticipation and nerves as well but chalked it up to the warehouse's bad acoustics just the same. "No, I'm coming. I can hear your voice . . . damn, this place is big!"

"Big place," he murmured, almost to himself as his voice echoed softly in reply. "Big ideas."

He turned a corner, gently, slowly, stretching out his anticipation until he saw her, radiant and flushed, dwarfed by the massive entryway with its cubist desks and funky wall art and bean bag waiting chairs. For once, there was no Spike ever at the ready, winking, nudging, and murmuring to spoil the reunion.

She wore a simple crinkle skirt, flowing and casual and as non-traditional as her breezy black tank top and matching sandals. It was such a bold and refreshing change after Jevon and Spike's holiday fashion show earlier in the day. To say she looked radiant was an understatement.

She looked, quite simply, tasty. A treat to devour again and again. The glow of her skin, the breezy black ponytail, and the expectant look in her eyes — all of it drew him in as easily as the vaulted ceilings and high walls of the massive warehouse.

Then he cocked his head curiously, realizing that something was missing. Something vital to her mission in Lakemont. "Hey, where's your big, fancy valise?"

She cocked her head back, a curious smile on her lips. Glanced at him curiously and replied saucily, "Whyever would I need that, big guy?"

He took her arm, a warm, almost embarrassed smile covering her face even as she gripped his hand seemingly nervously, and he began walking her back to the break room where they'd all brainstormed the day before. It was, as ever, the heart and soul of his company, and he reasoned that it was the nerve center of his brain trust.

The perfect place to take her tonight. "Isn't today your big pitch presentation?"

She shrugged, softly leaning into him as they walked, the soft sounds of Christmas music twinkling from a speaker near the microwave. "I'm done trying to win you over, Branch."

"I mean, you did that the minute you walked into my office two days ago."

She paused just as they rounded the corner to the clean lines and funky vibe of the employee break room. "No, I mean . . . wait, I did?"

He chuckled, rolling his eyes playfully even as they drifted gently away from each other at the snack bar entrance. "Stop. Of course you did."

Her mouth had opened to say one thing, it seemed, but peering upon the tableau before her made her say something else. "What . . . what is all this?"

He shrugged, suddenly bashful about his preparations. "I just thought you could use a treat. In all our, uh, time together, we haven't actually sat down and had a real meal."

Her face was red, but her gaze was intent as she peered across the breakroom bar at him. "Well, we tried that one night . . ."

"Well, let's try harder this time, shall we?"

She reached for the champagne bottle poking out of the ice bowl at the end of the countertop. "If you insist," she murmured, making herself at home and filling two of the plastic champagne flutes next to the bowl. He'd meant to be the perfect host, seating her and wining and dining her, but as always, her bossier, big city girl, do-it-all attitude got the best of him.

In only the best of ways, of course.

"I do, Avery," he said with a knowing wink. "For the time being, I insist that we try very, very hard to eat, drink and be merry."

"What's so urgent, anyway? And . . ." She turned, glass halfway to her lips, ripe and open, as her gaze scanned the dozens of strings of lights that illuminated the back of the warehouse itself. "When . . . when did you do all this?"

"I had a little free time today, so . . ." He let his gaze follow hers, admiring the decorations in real time right along with her. He had to say, they were quite impressive.

"It's so . . . Christmassy." She was walking along the back wall of the warehouse, sipping champagne absently as he followed.

"Well, it is . . . Christmas Eve."

"Right," she murmured, turning gently toward him, face aglow from the millions of lights just overhead. "I keep forgetting."

"I usually do."

"And now?"

They were standing face to face below the loft where he spent most sleepless nights, tossing and turning with new ideas and possibilities before he inevitably just got up, raced downstairs, and tapped them out on a notepad or two while waiting for the cappuccino machine to heat up. "Now? I just . . . wanted this year to be special."

She chuckled coyly, reaching in to flutter the fuzzy ball at the end of his droopy Santa hat, a last-minute addition the boys thought might add to the warehouse's festive glow. "So that's why the hat?"

"Something like that."

He gently guided her back toward the catered meal he'd asked the boys to order that same morning, platters of fruit and cheese, olives and sausage, *petit fours,* and chocolate-covered strawberries, and other treats too numerous and savory to mention. She nodded at the display, looking as impressed as she was curious.

"Is . . . the rest of the team coming?"

He chuckled, caught off guard by the question. Even he had to admit that it *was* a lot of food. "No, just us. I asked the boys to pick up a few things this morning, and, well . . . they kind of went overboard."

She grabbed a chocolate-covered strawberry, nibbling it sensuously while cooing and rolling her eyes in demonstration of its richness. "Well, at least they have good taste."

Her joyful nibble, followed by a gleeful sip of fine, dry champagne, seemed to give them both permission to dig in. They did so energetically, nibbling olives from toothpicks and filling little snowman-covered plates with grapes, mini-croissants, and other assorted treats. They found themselves at one of the plastic high-top tables, sitting across from each other, nibbling heartily like old friends and occasionally gingerly like new lovers.

She ate lustily, as she did most things, reminding him of the tomboy she'd always been back in school. The ivy league had toned her down a tad, and in her fine tailored suits and high heels, she looked every bit the lady.

But beneath the thin veneer and glossy city girl sheen, her hair was always just a stray lock away from coming down, her heels just a kick of her feet from coming off. He admired her ability to travel two worlds at once, adopting the vernacular and sheen of big-city life while remaining a small-town girl at heart.

Like the way she'd quickly taken control of the room while he and the kids had been brainstorming the day before. Statuesque and commanding in her fine linen suit, her easy charm, quick wit, and biting tongue had merged seamlessly until, moments into her presentation, she was both the leader of—and one of—a very demanding, commanding, prickly team.

He could likewise picture her pitching new clients, land developers, investors, or the sort, representing Archer Enterprises in a way he'd never been able to quite master. He was no slouch, to be sure, but he was more interested in making people happy than talking investors into something they weren't quite sure about. He noticed right away that Avery was not just a people mover but an *influencer*.

She'd inherited that much from her stepfather, at least.

They wound down at nearly the same time, smiling and satisfied as he savored the way her fingers gripped the cheap champagne flute and her lips graced the glass's rim. Her trademark black cherry lip gloss flowed seamlessly with her raven black hair to achieve the sultry, smoky effect he'd always favored. But even without makeup, she'd still been flawless to him.

He sat back in his molded plastic barstool, a vibrant yellow to match the eclectic, funky vibe of the open-air breakroom. He gave her a curious grin. "So you're really not gonna pitch me tonight, Avery?"

She shook her head almost somberly. Branch himself was vaguely disappointed. "Tomorrow, then?"

She squirmed gently in her own molded plastic seat, giving him a curious smirk. "No means no, Branch."

He sipped the last drop of champagne from his glass before topping them both off and sitting back with a well-earned sigh. "I just . . . isn't that what you came here to do, though?"

She seemed to consider the question and stared at the bubbles in her champagne longer than was necessary. "It's what I was sent here to do, Branch. There's . . . a difference." Their gazes met curiously over the cluttered table as she gently, almost absently, set her glass down. "I guess, I'm just realizing that now. As we speak."

He felt something change between them then. Something small, but significant. "So, what changed your mind?"

She gave another discerning pause before answering, with a wave of her hand at the lights above them, the table beneath them, and at the whole vibe and scene of the warehouse itself. "You, I guess. This place, for sure. The whole town and how it bears your fingerprint on every cool, funky, hip, successful thing in it. I just . . . Dad's company is about sucking creative people in and smoothing them out until they align with his narrow worldview that everything, and everyone, exists to make a profit."

She reached for her glass, seeing his face. "What? Why are you grinning like that?"

"I dunno. I guess . . . that's the first time this weekend you've referred to it as your dad's company and not . . . the family business." He made a dramatic face and wriggled spooky fingers to emphasize how serious she'd seemed when she first blew into town and how, gradually, hour by hour, perhaps even orgasm by orgasm, she'd eased back to what he hoped was her true nature.

Avery absently flicked at something unseen atop the lap of her gently flowing crinkle skirt. "I guess because it doesn't feel like a family business, you know? Not *my* family anyway."

"But it is your family, Avery."

She considered the statement carefully, if not pleasantly. "In name, I suppose. And I do feel a vague sense of loyalty to Archibald. He paid for my schooling, after all. My room and board and clothes allowance and . . ."

Branch gave her a gentle nudge of his own beneath the table. "I mean, you did get a hefty inheritance from your mother's side, Avery. It's not like you couldn't have paid that yourself."

She gave him a wry, knowing smile. "And how, pray-tell, did you know that little nugget?"

"You think I built all this without keeping abreast of current financial issues, Avery? I read the trades, and I hear the scuttlebutt. Your father isn't exactly publicity shy, you know?"

"I suppose. But Archibald taught me never to use my own money if someone else is willing to pay, and, well, he's always been willing to pay, so . . ."

Branch glanced away at a string of lights he could have wound tighter. She nudged him again. "What's that look for?"

He glanced back her way. "Nothing, I just . . . your father strikes me as the type who makes good investments."

"And?"

"Paying for your schooling, grooming you for success, making sure you had a good skill set before joining Balthazar Broadcasting just seems like a good investment, you know?"

Her crooked smile was both curious and wistful. "So I should be loyal? Or I shouldn't? I'm getting mixed messages here."

"I can't tell you what to do, Avery. I can only tell you what I see."

"Which is?" Avery picked up her champagne glass while she waited but didn't take a sip.

He shrugged. "Just that maybe I'm not the only asset in the room Archibald Balthazar is trying to acquire, you know?"

"I do know that, for sure. I've never forgotten it, either. I just . . . it's a little more personal for me, don't you think?"

He smirked. "I do know it's personal. And I do know that's why you, instead of one of his usual henchmen, were sent here to win me over."

"Which henchmen?"

Branch rolled his eyes. "You think this was the first pitch meeting from Balthazar Broadcasting I've endured, Avery?"

"It isn't?"

"I mean, it's been the most, uh . . . entertaining, but hardly the first."

Avery nibbled on the news the same way she'd sampled his early afternoon brunch treats. "I guess I shouldn't be surprised. You are one, uh . . . attractive asset, Branch."

He eased back into the seat at his back, luxuriating in the view. "You're not so bad yourself, hot pants."

She chuckled hoarsely — God, how he loved that sound — and glanced almost bashfully away.

"Still, Avery, you were sent here on a mission. I . . . I don't want you to go back to your stepfather empty-handed."

She rolled her eyes and nudged his shin beneath the table. "Just who's side are you on, anyway?"

"Yours, obviously. I just know how . . . convincing . . . your father can be."

She looked him up and down, another move of hers that

was sure to make him shiver in all the right places. "He obviously hasn't convinced you yet."

"So . . . what now?"

She frowned, and even that was beautiful. "I guess I'll cross that bridge when I come to it."

"When? Tomorrow?"

Their gazes met across the crowded table, littered with empty glasses and balled-up snowman napkins. She merely nodded.

He quietly stood. She watched him reach for the bottle on the nearby table and return. "You don't have to go, you know?"

"I do, actually," she muttered, glancing away for the first time.

He filled her glass, still standing as he set the bottle down on the resin tabletop. "You . . . don't, actually."

CHAPTER TWENTY-NINE: AVERY

"Do tell, Branch."

He winked, turning to the whiteboard they'd brainstormed on the other day. It was blank again, but he waved a dry-erase marker in his right hand as if ready to change that fairly soon. Avery watched him move casually, easily, around the break room space he literally, but also figuratively, owned.

He looked so natural in his home environment, casually radiant in his daily attire, and clearly comfortable in what had become his natural habitat. She smirked to think her father could ever swoop in and snatch such an organic, cohesive, clearly caring company from the very man that had created it out of thin air.

He gave her a knowing glance. "I'd prefer to show, actually."

She rolled her eyes, even as her belly quivered in anticipation. She'd always considered herself a fairly independent woman, king of her own castle, master of her own domain, but something about Branch had her eager to see if maybe he could find a route out of her current predicament in a way she simply couldn't, try as she might.

Or, perhaps, she simply wouldn't.

Branch was, after all, an idea man.

"So," he began, drawing a circle in the middle of the empty board. "Here was Lakemont when we both grew up here. Boring. Stale. Bland. Nothing to do, nowhere to go, little to eat." He began adding dots, squares, and triangles all around the circle. "I've been busy changing that while you were, you know, away being studious and sexy and brilliant, but . . . there's something missing . . ."

He began drawing arrows from each of the shapes bordering the circle to the middle, still empty. "And I didn't know what it was until you showed up the other day."

He glanced over at her, winking as he drew a big, stupid, uneven heart in the middle. The marker squeaked across the dry-erase board, as charming as it was flattering. "Branch, seriously . . ."

He tapped the heart in the middle, leaving little black specks inside every time he did so. "I mean it, Avery. I saw you with those kids yesterday. They're a tough crowd, very protective of our world-building here, and they welcomed you with open arms. Why? Because you're smart, capable, can read the room, and process information quickly."

"You already have a room full of geniuses to help you do that, Branch. You don't need me."

"You're exactly what I need," he said, waving the pen dramatically. "Sure, the kids and I have ideas and vision, but sometimes we lack focus. Guardrails. We all like the same things and tend to pile on when an idea is good, and even when it's not so good. We love what we do, and we love each other, and that doesn't always troubleshoot ideas as thoroughly as I'd like. What I saw yesterday helped pull that into clearer focus, and this is coming from a guy who always thinks he's right, so . . ."

She crossed her arms over her chest, struggling not to get caught up in his boyish enthusiasm. "So you're looking for a den mother, basically?"

Branch's face fell, as if he thought she was kidding. "Are you . . . even listening to me?" He tapped the board again, even though he was staring straight at her. "Focus now. I'm looking for a partner, Avery. Someone I can trust, who I can grow this company with into the future."

She clucked a tongue. "That's exactly the pitch my stepfather wanted to give *you*, Branch."

"This isn't a pitch, Avery. I'm not asking you to work under me or for me. I'm asking you to work *with* me."

"Branch, I have an apartment back in Manhattan. A job. An office, a . . ." Avery sputtered to make any sense, her excuses sounding lame even as they left her helpless mouth.

He set the dry-erase marker down in the little tray at the bottom of the whiteboard. Inched closer wearing a triumphant smile. "Funny, Avery," he murmured, as menacing as he was endearing. "You didn't say you had a life back in Manhattan."

"Oh, like I have one here?"

"You did once, remember?" He wasn't backing down, no matter what excuses she lobbed back at him. If anything, he seemed to be *doubling* down.

"I do remember, Branch. I remember feeling like a stranger here, even when it was my home."

He nodded, covering her hands with his. For once, her reaction wasn't to flinch or pull away. For once, for now, she was still hoping for a solution.

"To me, Avery, it always felt like you were struggling to find out who you really were. Even now, I can't tell if you're here on personal or professional terms. This . . . this is a second chance for you. To come home, to be home, to feel at home."

"With you, you mean?"

"With us, Avery."

She squeezed his hand in reply, then abruptly stood, eager to rid herself of the nervous energy that had consumed her all day. "Branch, this *us* is temporary, you know that, right?"

He gave her back as good as he got. "I know that, Avery. I get that. I'm grown. So are you. We both have choices, and I may be grasping at straws at the moment. But right now, I'm the only one in the room acting like he knows that."

"I have choices."

His tone, his posture, his gaze, it was all one big challenge. "So choose, then."

"What, Branch? Tonight?"

"It'd be nice, yeah."

"You sound just like the kids who work for you."

"And what's so wrong with that?"

"Nothing, except that we're not eighteen anymore."

"We're not fifty, either, Avery. You act like your life is already over. Like you have no choice but to return to Manhattan and work for your father until you succeed him some thirty, forty years down the line. Decades and decades of pitching companies and buying companies and picking apart companies to fit into your stepfather's narrow view of what entertainment really means. There's another way, Avery."

"For you, maybe. For you, Branch. But . . . not for me."

Branch looked crestfallen.

She knew how he felt. She surveyed the scene, the lights, the tree, the breakroom, the stockings, the music, the cheer, the champagne, and her gut ached with the remorse and regret of it all.

He'd done exactly what she'd wanted and tried his best to change her mind. In the end, only she could do that. And for some reason, she just wasn't ready yet.

She took an involuntary step backward, distancing herself from his enthusiasm, his excitement, his dreamy-eyed pitch. "I'm sorry, Branch. I've ruined your Christmas."

He frowned, lying through his teeth. "No you didn't, Avery. It was . . . ambitious of me to think you'd give up everything you have to join me here."

His words might have sounded soothing, but even a salesman like Branch couldn't hide the abject disappointment in his voice.

Even as the walls of her decision closed in on her, blotting out the gaily winking lights and festive atmosphere, she struggled to keep a brave tone to her voice. "I won't say it's not tempting."

"Sure, Avery. Sure. Just . . . not tempting enough."

"I didn't say that, either, Branch. I just . . . don't know what to say."

His eyes widened, nodding at her slow, gradual departure. "Will you sleep on it, at least?"

She sighed, glancing around the breakroom one last time before inching past it, and turning back toward the main entrance. "I doubt I'll do much sleeping tonight, Branch. And I leave in the morning, so . . ."

He followed her, just slightly behind.

"Just, at least promise me you'll consider it?"

When she didn't answer right away, when she couldn't quite answer, he grabbed her wrist, turning her gently in the funky vibe of the colorful warehouse foyer. "Please, as . . . as a Christmas present to me?"

His boyish request, his earnest sincerity, the crack in his voice like he was still going through puberty, was a far more effective pitch than any circles or squares he'd scribbled on the dry-erase board. For the first time, for the first *real* time, she was actually considering his utterly ludicrous, absolutely ridiculous idea. "For Christmas, Branch. Sure."

He seemed so relieved that his hand was visibly trembling as he opened the big metal door for her. She gently grabbed his wrist. "And for my present, Branch? Will you . . . promise not to be disappointed if I make the wrong choice?"

He frowned, struggling to seem playful. "I'll meet you halfway, Avery. I'll promise not to *act* disappointed, okay? That's the best I can do."

"I'll take it, then," she murmured, already drifting past him to the parking lot. The sky was dark now, the neon marquee letters above the door favoring Branch's youthful, still hopeful face.

She idly wondered, reaching for her bike in the bike stand, if she was up for it. If she could actually disappoint him. If she could crush the hopeful look in his eyes after all he'd done to convince her otherwise. Avery had come to the warehouse looking for answers, for solutions, and she left with only more questions.

CHAPTER THIRTY: BRANCH

"Bah humbug."

Branch rose from a fitful few hours of sleep, knowing before he glanced at his phone that the hour would be ungodly, and not disappointed to glance outside his loft window to see it still cripplingly dark outside.

3:23 AM.

Christmas, officially.

Bah. Fucking. Humbug.

Now he knew why he never celebrated the season in the first place. Branch had been raised by a single father, his mother having fled the scene shortly after his second birthday. He had no memories of her and only a few scattered *Polaroids* his father had taken of them together during happier, more chaotic times. None of her and Branch together. Not one. His father had been a smoker. And a drinker. And a gambler. And a scoundrel. And a lay about, lazy, stinkin' bum.

Not a bad guy, exactly. Just weak and unmotivated and in the end, selfish to the core. Branch had been a nerd in high school because books, music, comics, movies . . . they were escapes he could indulge in while his father smoked and drank his way through the rent and food money most months. They bounced from house to house, apartment to apartment, trailer to trailer until Branch was old enough to get a job at a local diner and begin making money all his own.

To control his father's bad habits, Branch started giving the old man an allowance every week. Things stabilized by the time he'd gotten to high school, but not for long. His father

162

got sick and never quite recovered, a combination of bad habits and bad genetics that took him far too soon. At the very least, Branch had consoled himself at the time that the old man was out of whatever misery had made him so constantly unhappy during his brief time on this planet.

The only thing his father left him was an old insurance policy that he'd somehow, magically, almost miraculously, managed to pay the premium on even in the worst of times. With the proceeds of that single payout, Branch bought his first *restaurant*, a hot dog stand that was going out of business. It was situated between a liquor store and a check cashing place and had been struggling for years.

Branch closed it down for a few weeks after buying it, hired a few local handymen, and reopened it as a *monster malt shop* he'd cheekily named the *Creature Café*. He'd long seen a need for something that would appeal to all the baby boomers and retirees who made up most of the population of scenic, if dull, Lakemont, California. But that it would also be unique enough, charming enough, creative enough, and even entertaining enough, to stand out.

In addition to gleaming new ovens for the refurbished kitchen and napkin holders for the café tables, Branch had invested in a dozen or so old monster movie posters, a few cheap props he'd found on eBay, and enough old black and white monster movie DVDs to play on an endless loop while the folks who'd grown up watching them shoved greasy fries, sizzling burgers, and thick malted shakes down their gizzards all day.

It was an instant success and a wildly popular idea whose time had finally come. The Boomers came in droves, then brought their children, then their grandchildren, sharing a love of old black and white monster movies and more innocent times with their extended families.

In less than a year, he'd bought the shops on either side of the original diner and expanded the *Creature Café* to three times its size, and still, the place was standing room only from breakfast through dinner seven days a week. The following year he bought the strip mall itself, turning the other half-dozen stores into old-timey, retro, vintage outlets to include a monster-movie-themed gift shop, a DVD rental business, and even a monster-themed candy store.

In so doing, Branch had discovered the power behind nostalgia. He'd started with the 50s, black and white, monster movie malt shoppe, and penny candy vibe, but quickly moved onto the 60s with another strip mall investment he quickly fitted out with vinyl record stores, vintage thrift shops, and a retro lounge featuring lava lamps, glow in the dark posters and Jimi Hendrix and the Doors music blasting nonstop.

With each new success, he invested in something new, the 70s disco and roller rink vibe, the 80s video and fashion vibe, and the 90s music and gadget vibe until, at last, he'd cornered the market on all things retro.

Along the way, he'd managed to entertain — and feed — entire generations of families, growing as they grew, adopting and adapting to each new desire as he amassed a talented, energetic, youthful team to help him shape each new venture with all the nostalgia boxes checked.

And, after all that, he would trade it all, his whole damn empire, every single penny of profit, for another single night with Avery. He knew, as he finally rose from his bed, bare feet on hardwood floors, that he was only slightly exaggerating.

Very, very slightly.

He'd left the romantic scene set from the night before, jar candles on every available surface of his loft area, gently flickering in the dark of night even as the Christmas lights glowed gently along the metal walkway that surrounded his long, narrow loft on the warehouse's second floor.

He grabbed a can of iced coffee from the dorm fridge under the nightstand by his bed, sipping it slowly as he paced the long, narrow walkway overlooking the fruits of his labor down below.

He was restless even before the caffeine hit and positively fidgety by the time he'd finished the tall, slim can and tossed it into the recycling bin by his dresser. He'd given up on changing Avery's mind the minute she'd left the warehouse the night before, not even bothering to watch her pedal away as he closed the door on whatever he thought they might have had together.

And the longer he stewed, pacing around the break room, then up and down the stairs, rolling his eyes at the old-timey Christmas music and shaking his head at how quickly she'd shut him down, he realized he'd been a fool for even trying in the first place.

Sure, he'd been successful in his endeavors, and the vibe at the Archer Enterprise warehouse was fun, friendly, and funky, but could millions possibly compete with the billions her father had to offer at some point down the line? He'd gone to bed feeling foolish, and frankly, embarrassed that he'd tried so hard to break down a wall that was far too high for him to scale in the first place.

Suddenly, panic-stricken, he realized his error.

He'd been negotiating deals since that very first hot dog stand turned *Creature Café*. He knew better than to let the customer sway the conversation, which was exactly what Avery had done, whether either of them had realized it at the time or not. He'd begged her to consider his option when, instead, he should have demanded she do so.

Sure, she might have been some badass, ball-busting city girl, but only in theory. Everything he'd seen, heard, tasted, and plundered since she'd arrived in town told Brach that Avery could be swayed with just the right kind of . . .

guidance.

He chuckled, embarrassed by his naivete, tossing off various garments as he fled into the hot, comforting spray of a middle-of-the-night shower. The best kind, in his opinion. He dried himself and dressed quickly, casually, blowing out candles along the way and wishing he hadn't lit quite so many. He was positively out of breath by the time he reached for the warehouse door.

And hell, he still had to ride across town . . .

CHAPTER THIRTY-ONE: AVERY

"What took you so long, Nerd?"

Branch beamed, literally skidding to a stop on his sleek yellow beach cruiser as he rolled up to the streamlined façade of Avery's old house. His face registered confusion, even through his gleeful, boyish smile. "What . . . what are you doing out here?"

She shrugged, lounging in one of the folding beach chairs she'd found in one corner of the otherwise empty garage. The door was open behind her, Christmas music oozing quietly on a portable speaker just out of sight. She patted the second deck chair, glad her father's assistant had thought to buy two when preparing for her arrival that weekend.

"Waiting for your tardy ass to show up, Branch. That's what."

He stood from the bike, face aglow and chest gently heaving. He looked like he'd been in a road race of some sort, and her heart fluttered to think Branch might have hurried across town just to see little old her.

"In . . . in the middle of the night?" He finally sank into his seat, the heat swimming off him in waves. Delightfully tempting, delicious waves of heat and his telltale masculine musk.

God, how she'd missed that smell.

And oh, how she craved it anew.

"It's not really night if you never went to sleep in the first place, Branch."

"You either?"

"I wanted to be good and ready when you came to your

senses, you big dummy." She patted the cooler between them, chilled and ready. "You up for a little more bubbly to continue our, uh, negotiations?"

He looked delightfully, deliciously confused. "You don't have to ask me twice."

She shivered in anticipation, raw and clearly undisguised, as the sounds of shifting ice and a popping cork made her wince with unreserved pleasure and shudder with ripe, poorly cloaked desire. Hell, she might as well have been sitting there bare-ass naked to the world.

Which she'd seriously considered, actually.

Before coming to her senses, that was.

There were cupholders in the canvas deck chairs, cups already inside. He wasn't the only one who could put on a good holiday spread at the last minute, she thought wryly, watching him aglow and radiant beneath the December moonlight. Branch noticed, filled them quickly, and gently set the bottle back down on the cooler as if it might break.

Or perhaps he thought anything more forceful might simply break the mood. "Bubbly is appropriate," he murmured, clinking her paper cup before taking a soft, appreciative sip.

"Sure, I mean, it's Christmas officially . . ."

He reached for something in his pocket, revealing a manilla envelope. "No, I mean, we have a reason to celebrate."

She nodded as if perhaps he was suddenly hard of hearing. "Yeah, Christmas."

"No, silly, I . . . just open it."

Avery did just that. She'd expected a Christmas card. Maybe a gift card from one of the local convenience stores still open at this ungodly hour. Instead, she saw a stock certificate, instantly recognizable and looking just like the hundreds she already had for Balthazar Broadcasting, courtesy of her mother's divorce settlement and, eventually, last will and testament.

This one, however, was for . . . Archer Enterprises.

She shook her head emphatically. "Branch, I . . ."

He nodded twice as hard. "Just stop, Avery." His voice was a low, guttural, commanding growl. "It's Christmas. It's a gift. Take it."

"How . . . how did you get it notarized this late? Or, should I say, so early?"

"My lawyer lives in town. She owes me a few . . . favors."

"Favors?" Avery murmured, a sudden flare of irrational jealousy forcing a blush to her face. "Do I want to know?"

"Gross, not that kind! Let's just say you would've had a few more shares if I hadn't had to throw her a couple for the last-minute seal of approval on Christmas Day, okay?"

"Branch, ninety-nine shares or a hundred. You know I can't accept any of them."

He was far less amenable than he'd been back in the warehouse. "Of course you can, you big stubborn dork. You helped name my next business venture, were integral in the planning stage, and even branded a few key theme nights in the process. This is . . . consider them hush shares."

"Hush shares? I'm . . . MBA or no, I'm not familiar with the term."

"You know, so you won't sue me when the new drive-thru opens and uses all those great ideas you gave us."

She chuckled, butterflies dancing in her belly amidst the delightfully quick buzz of fresh champagne bubbles. "How soon are you planning on opening, anyway?"

"Why, you wanna cash them in already?"

"No, but . . ." Avery waved the expertly wrapped present her father had left on her counter for emphasis. "I might need a job soon."

Branch literally, comically, almost spit out his champagne. "Come again?"

She handed him the long, thin box. "What, you think you're the only man in my life to give me presents on Christmas? For the first year ever, I'm apparently in big demand!"

He opened the box. Took out the top sheet of paper, a simple paragraph full of her father's scrawling cursive centered just so on a crisp, formal sheet of instantly familiar Balthazar Broadcasting stationary. He scanned it quickly, then squinted for a better, longer look. All the same, he was grinning ear to ear when he remarked, "He fired you? On Christmas Day?"

She shrugged and sipped more champagne, surprisingly resigned to the surreal nature of the moment. Stock shares. Letter of termination. Champagne. Branch. In her frickin' driveway in the middle of the damn night, no less. She wouldn't have been surprised if Santa himself had whizzed by tossing down presents from atop his sleigh to cap things off. "Christmas Eve, technically, but . . . short version, sure. Yes."

Branch glanced at the memo and narrowed his eyes, pointing at a particular line toward the end. "What does he mean by *your next endeavor*, Avery?"

She grinned. She'd already memorized the three or four succinct lines shortly after reading them, heart in her throat, palms steadily shaking,

Avery Reedy Balthazar is hereby terminated from all duties and responsibilities at Balthazar Broadcasting. Her foundling division, Themed Eateries and Entertainment, is hereby disbanded forthwith. Her stock shares and monthly stipend remain intact indefinitely, per previous agreements. See attached for financial specifics.

We wish her all the luck in her next endeavor and will continue to monitor her progress from the home office.

She smirked, shoulders light and heart free with the sudden release of pressure she'd been feeling since graduating and moving into her unfurnished office at Balthazar

Broadcasting HQ. "You, I suppose."

"Me?"

Avery nodded, topping off their glasses as she squirmed in supreme satisfaction in her canvas chair. "I think he got the picture when I didn't come back from Lakemont the day after I arrived, you — and your company — in tow. Or maybe when I went incommunicado for two days, and he had to text me a last-minute *SOS* to make sure I was still alive. Or perhaps when he had to step over the boxer briefs you left in my kitchen to leave that term letter on my counter. Either way, I guess he got the message."

Brach either ignored the more salacious details of her hasty explanation or was simply too focused on the moment at hand to care. "So now what?"

Avery sighed and glanced out past the driveway at the peacefully, almost gaily, lit streets of her old neighborhood. "Nothing for a while, I guess. I got a generous severance package, of course. Stocks, percentages, consulting fees, that kind of thing. Plus, he included the deed to the house we're sitting in front of, so . . . financially, I'm good. More than good. I just . . ."

Her voice tapered off.

Branch apparently noticed. Winked. "It was never just financial for you anyway, right, Avery? You need a little creative boost to keep your motors humming, huh?"

"After a few days, sure. I'm gonna be climbing these walls pretty soon."

He waved his champagne cup merrily. "Well, my offer still stands."

"Good, because . . ."

"The best part is, the kids don't come back until after the New Year, so . . . we'll have time to brainstorm a little until then."

"Brainstorm?"

"Yeah, you know . . ." His hand drifted out, dragging her crinkle skirt gently above one knee as she murmured with delight, the cool morning air soothing her suddenly feverish skin. "We'll need to brainstorm how to relive a few more of those fantasies we've been exploring this weekend."

"Such as?"

"Such as . . ." Branch chuckled, making her wilt inside even as she pressed her thigh deeper into the heat of his palm. "Let's start with those walls you wanted to climb?"

CHAPTER THIRTY-TWO: BRANCH

"**B**ranch, I . . ."

Avery gasped, her back pressed against the foyer wall, his hands pinning her shoulders in place as he silenced her with a breathless kiss.

His hands were all over her, tugging and pulling at the black tank top and shimmery gray skirt. Hers did the same, wrenching up the hem of his V-neck tee even as she yanked at the button of his pants. Already hard, his straining erection threatened to knock her back into the kitchen counter if she let it free so soon.

"No, I . . ." She gasped, shaking her way out of his ravenous kiss and struggling to refill her desperately aching lungs. Somehow, she squirmed from his grasp, leaving him leaning against the living room wall as she righted her skirt and one strap of her top. "It's my turn to fantasize, remember?"

"Are you positive? Because I've been keeping track, and I'm not sure your calculations are correct this time."

She chuckled, grabbing his hand and leading him toward the bedroom. He went so willingly that he almost overtook her. "Does it matter?"

His laugh was rich and thick, and he felt it all the way to his throbbing, aching hard-on. "Guess not. I just . . . already have a few in mind, that's all."

"Same, bud, same, but . . . we've got all week, remember, so . . . me first."

"Fine, if you insist."

"Oh, trust me," she murmured, turning suddenly to whisper in his ear. "You won't be disappointed."

She wasn't kidding. In no time, he was on her bed, flat on his back as she squirmed atop his shuddering belly, the heat from between her legs threatening to sear his very flesh. She tugged mercilessly at his cotton t-shirt, dragging it off and over his head as Branch struggled to contain his excitement. It wasn't easy, not when she casually stripped off her slinky black tank top to expose those stiff, tasty nipples before leaning forward and extending his hand to one corner of the wrought iron headboard.

"Now, just lie still," she cautioned, tying his right hand with the tank top even as her ripe rump wriggled against the tip of his leaking prick. She used his shirt to tie the other wrist to the opposite end of the headboard, fastening him tightly so that, even as he struggled, he couldn't break free.

Not that he wanted to, of course. If anything, he found the sudden loss of freedom . . . freeing. Last time it had been Branch's turn to take control and pound her into a writhing frenzy of face-down lust. Eagerly, he handed over the reins and couldn't wait to see how she would take him this time.

"Is this your fantasy or mine?" he murmured, suddenly breathless as she slithered the skirt up and over her head, revealing sheer nakedness beneath. No wonder his belly was slathered with her excitement, her wet, obvious heat that tempted and teased his cock with its fiery furnace, so close and yet so far.

"You wore that to the warehouse last night?" Branch shook his head, gulping at the missed opportunity. "Or, should I say, didn't wear that?"

She playfully murmured, her pussy slick atop his taut belly. Jesus, she was damp. Wetter, hotter, and slicker than she'd ever been before.

"Why do you think I was so pissed when I left, Branch?"

"That was you being pissed?"

She shrugged, the motion rippling through her firm, petite breasts and making him lick his lips. As if to tease him all the more, she reached up and untethered her trademark ponytail, flawlessly straight black hair cascading atop her shoulders in reply. "In my way, sure."

"Well, maybe if I'd known you weren't wearing panties, I would have gotten to the pleasure before the business."

Her hand reached down, stroking him greedily through the thin layer of his boxer briefs, the only clothes she'd left in place. "Better late than never, Branch."

"You can say that again," he gasped as she made quick work of tugging them down past his knees.

She slithered playfully away, shimmering across his cock with her ripe, wet lips before their feet curled around one another's. Her breath was hot and enticing above his happy trail.

"What's that?" she cooed playfully, sticking out her tongue to lap at the moisture dotting his own quivering tip. "That's gonna be hard to do with my mouth full, big boy."

No sooner had she finished the quip than she made good on her promise, savoring the meaty tip of his glistening cock with more fervor than ever before. Fully committing to the fantasy, he gripped the wrought iron bars of the headrest with eager fingers and white knuckles, straining less against his bonds than he did with the urge to blast his way through the approaching orgasm that threatened to end this fantasy before it even began.

She seemed to sense it, cooing even as she slid him playfully from between her plump, glistening lips.

"Not yet, lover," she murmured, stroking him slowly as if bringing him down gently from Cloud-nine. If only she knew the sensation of her wet, greedy fingers on his sopping dick was nearly just as pleasurable as the sucking sensation of her expert lips on his glistening staff.

In time she left him to his own devices, wriggling back up the length of his splayed-out body until her throbbing clit pulsed and poked at his belly. She guided him in, gently, then less so, until they both heard the noisy, sexy *thwack* of insertion, and he shuddered at the intense pleasure of slithering back inside her tight, clingy pussy.

Her eyes fluttered, no longer coy but eagerly, hungrily sensual. She slid her hands up his arms until they clasped his fingers and then began to ride him in earnest, grinding her poignant bud eagerly against the base of his cock as he plunged deeper and deeper inside with every thrust and parry.

His hands might have been bound to the headboard and this might have been her fantasy, but he was not without recourse. He gradually spread his legs, forcing a moan of pleasure from deep inside her as he ground gently deeper with the new angle. All the same, she whimpered and murmured as her body begged for more.

He gave it to her, sliding his feet up the bed and bending gently at the knee as he began to lift his ass up off the bed, plunging harder, faster, and, yes, deeper inside. She gasped, gripped his hands, and bucked wildly with the release of a sudden, unexpected, but no less powerful orgasm.

He felt the walls of her pussy tighten and throb even as he yearned to do the same. Still, somehow, he resisted, riding out the waves of her tender explosion until her screams became whimpers, her cries growing hoarser, and then, and only then, did he pulse and pound her into another gasping, shuddering orgasm.

He thrust, and she ground.

He grunted, and she groaned.

She came faster now, the cycles closing in on themselves until she was eventually one continuous, clenching vibration of sweat and tight, gritty lust. He pumped less and simply remained wedged in tight, deep to the hilt, skin against feverish skin and gently grinding and pressing from left to right in time to her colorful bursts of ecstasy. Branch moaned until he could resist no longer and pulled himself out as slowly and romantically as he dared, he pulsed and jerked until the blast coated and lathered Avery's already sweaty back.

She fell against him, collapsing atop his pounding chest even as his cock pulsed and leaked and splattered her quivering cheeks.

"Jesus," they murmured in unison, skin to skin, her hands gently releasing his even as she reached to untie him.

"No," he insisted desperately, still hungry for the taste of her despite the intensity of their lovemaking. "Not yet."

She chuckled, almost nervously, certainly hesitantly, lifting herself up just enough to glance down at him curiously. "You're a certified stud, Branch, but you're no teenager. You don't want to stay tied up until you're ready again."

She winked teasingly, giving her rump a saucy little shake as if to emphasize how splattered and drained he really was. "Your hands might lose all circulation, and, well, what good would they be to me then?"

"Forget my hands," he urged, their eyes meeting in the dim light of the humid bedroom even as he lifted himself up on his haunches to gently slither and slide her progress along his still shuddering belly. "Come closer, Avery. My lips are more than ready."

She shook her head, looking uncertain, biting her lower lip in hesitant uncertainty. "Branch, really, I'm fine . . ."

He gave her a good-natured growl, raising himself up higher to further her progress toward his desperate, hungry mouth. "You've had your fantasy, hot pants. This one's all mine." He thrust gently, inching her further up his belly as she slid atop his flat gut. "Come on, almost there . . ."

Chapter Thirty-three: Avery

"Are you sure?"

Branch licked his lips as if to prove it, making Avery blush harder than she already was, and not just in her face. Yet even as she asked, Avery slid her throbbing, almost achingly hot bud across his long taffy body, writhing with pleasure and anticipation as she steadied herself, palms out on either side of his chest, and brazenly guided his face between her thighs.

She would have refused any other man's request, especially after the heavenly pounding he'd just given her and the way she'd mined every drop of his lust from his pulsing prick. It was a craven, almost greedy act at this point, gilding the lily, as her mother always said, but damn . . . he made it sound so tasty and divine, and after all, it was Branch. They'd seen each other inside and out this weekend, and besides, what was a little face-planting between friends? She'd certainly tasted the best of him in the last few days. What was good for the goose, she reasoned, was good for the gander. And it was Christmas, after all.

Branch's tongue really was the gift that kept on giving.

She could already feel his breath, ragged and heavy, wash across her sodden lips even as she wriggled higher up the length of him. His lips were wet and full, eyes wide as she wriggled into place, and she felt the first damp sting of his puffy lips across her inner thigh.

"Jesus," she gushed, still quivering from the orgasms he'd already given her, and so help her, greedy as sin for a half-dozen more. "God," she gasped, his lips wet and full on the other thigh. Her skin was so sensitive that merely kissing her inner thigh sent spasms of pleasure through her body. Despite the urgency of his words, Branch seemed in no hurry, content to merely kiss and lick her glistening moisture from every inch he could reach, making her blush anew even as she thrilled to the erotic sensation of his mouth on her skin.

She crept closer still, greedier now than ever, even greedier than when she'd had him wedged deep inside and pressing gently as she still cried out for more.

At last she was close enough, spread wide enough to feel his lips smother and slather her tender clit with heat and moisture and a firmness that only came from sitting on her lover's face.

She came immediately, intensely, as much from the pleasure of his actions as the sheer, wanton, illicitness of it all. Even in her most debauched sorority days, which had always seemed rather chaste compared to her sisters' sex lives, she'd never dared smother a man's face with her wet, swollen pussy lips.

But Branch was savoring the experience, writhing and grinding his bare ass into the mattress as he sucked, licked, and murmured his way across her greedy pussy. She came and came, again and again, no longer hesitant but fully embracing the fantasy they both shared.

When sweat dripped freely from her skin, when her thighs trembled to the point of paralysis, and her belly ached from the sexual tension, when her throat was hoarse from calling out his name, and she knew to cum again would be to spend the rest of the day on the bench and out of whatever fantasy he might cook up next, she forced herself to drift gently away from his firm, expert chin and devilish tongue.

She lay atop him, his heart pounding as much as hers, face to face until she could no longer resist a kiss across those swollen, sticky lips. The taste was warm, wet, and musky and forbidden and sexy.

As.

Hell.

He knew it, murmuring, smiling, their tongues clashing as the last of her illicit desire mounted, and she ground her engorged clit atop one bony hip until the sexy sensation proved her undoing.

She came one last time, biting down playfully on his lower lip and squealing in his ear before she slid, helpless and sweaty, into a heap beside him.

Merry Christmas indeed . . .

CHAPTER THIRTY-FOUR: BRANCH

"A little help?"

Branch squirmed with the promise of relief finally at hand. Avery chuckled at his predicament, rubbing the sleep out of her eyes as, finally, sun caressed her blinking eyelids and puffy lips through the open blinds.

"Shit, sorry," she murmured, undoing his bonds as she apologized profusely, stifling a giggle. "I must have dozed off for a minute."

"Me, too, but . . ." The minute his bonds were freed, Branch leapt from the bed, leaving her giggling as he relieved himself for what felt like the next five minutes.

"You and your damn champagne." He chuckled, drying his hands as he stood in the glow of the bathroom door, peering down at her radiant, dew-dappled body and threatening to grow hard all over again.

The sun caressed her naked skin, her slept-on hair framing her angelic face as if on purpose. Shadows danced across her curves and angles, favoring her long, tapered legs and soft, rosy nipples as he made no secret of devouring every inch of her with his still hungry eyes.

She lay back, smirking up at him in all her sexy glory as if she knew the fire growing steadily in his belly. She drank him in, inch by saucy inch, admiring him in much the same way he'd admired her.

"Speaking of champagne . . ." Her voice, low and cautious, was as hoarse as a late-nigh radio DJ's, and Branch thought he might have never heard anything sexier in his life. It perfectly matched the slinky curves and coy, sexy look in her smoky green eyes.

"Great minds think alike," he purred, reaching for the closest garment he could find, his wrinkled, sweaty t-shirt, before wrapping it around his waist for the quick trip out to the kitchen. He wasn't sure why he bothered at this point. He'd never known a woman as intimately, as closely, as he'd known Avery Balthazar, and certainly, no woman had ever seen every inch of him the same way she had by now. To cover himself seemed silly at this point, and yet, old habits died hard, he supposed.

Branch opened the fridge, cold air slathering his feverish skin as he peered inside. There, on the top shelf, was another bottle of bubbly, cold, green, and inviting. He idly wondered how long a body could survive on sex and champagne and promised himself he would try his damndest to find out this very holiday.

Branch returned to the bedroom, bare feet on the hardwood floors, as he popped the cork in the bedroom doorway, watching it fly and zing halfway across the room. He sucked the foam off his finger and drank freely from the bottle, savoring the blend of bubbly and sweet, fleshy musk as he swallowed them both down with aplomb.

"No glasses?" she teased, sitting up by now and cross-legged, patting the bed at her feet.

"The bottle's glass," he mocked, handing it over. She shrugged and slid those soft, tempting lips around the top before slaking her thirst greedily, even lustily.

He mimicked her posture, both of them sitting on opposite edges of the bed, cross-legged, as if there might have been a campfire between them.

She gave him the bottle back. He sipped. Returned the favor. She was radiant, pale, and pink in all the right places, and despite having had her half a dozen times that weekend, he couldn't stop staring back at her.

Wanting her half a dozen, a dozen, a hundred times more. "You're beautiful," he murmured, waving the half-empty bottle at her. "You know that?"

She jutted out her chin bravely even as the cautious, even bashful look in her eyes didn't quite match the gesture. "I only know it when you look at me like that, Branch."

His reply was as naked as his glance. "I don't know how to look at you any other way, Avery."

She blushed, took the bottle, and quaffed heavily. "Do you promise to always look at me that way, Branch?"

He crossed his heart, half to honor her request, the other half to snatch the bottle from her greedy clutches. "Always, Avery. You have my word."

He handed her back the bottle. She sighed contentedly and leaned against the headboard at her back, a stack of ruffled pillows cushioning her from the wrought iron frame. She was still, as ever, resplendently, unabashedly naked. He slid closer, only slightly, until their knees gently touched. She smiled, nodding at him. "You sure you want me around all the time?"

He clucked his tongue as if she'd just asked the dumbest question ever. "I've *never* not wanted that, Avery Balthazar."

Despite his protestations, she still managed to look doubtful. "As a partner, I mean."

He sighed, spreading his legs and tugging himself closer, drawing her thighs atop his until they were groin to groin yet again. He felt her heat, but that wasn't why he'd done it. He clutched her face, kissing her lips gently, almost chastely, before leaning slightly back. "All the fantasies we've shared this weekend, Avery, and all the fantasies still to come, you wanna know what the biggest one is?"

She shook her head, eyes dewy, lips puffy, and looking all of ten years old. "The biggest fantasy of all, Avery, is that you'd join me at the warehouse. On the daily. On the nightly. Burning the midnight oil, conceiving, imagining, honing, and creating. Together. That's what I've been fantasizing about since graduation. And this chance you've given me? This second chance? I told myself, no matter what, this time, I wouldn't waste it."

She nodded, eyes moist as she reached out and drew him closer. It was a simple, but surprisingly tender gesture. For all her feminine ways, Avery Balthazar wasn't necessarily the touchy-feely type. To feel her gentle skin against his own, her hands clutching him tighter, was more romantic than any mere sex act.

"Thank you, Branch." Her voice was still a hoarse croak, now just above a whisper.

"For what?"

She glanced down at her lap abashedly. "For . . . not giving up on me."

"Thank *you*, Avery." He tilted her chin up so they could see eye to eye.

She cocked her head slightly. "For what, Branch?"

He smirked. "For waiting for me to come to my senses, obviously."

She chuckled, tears rolling down her blushing cheeks. He kissed them away, softly, gently, the moment stretching out in the quiet stillness of her sultry bedroom.

By the time his softly nudging kisses reached her gently parted lips, Branch wasn't surprised to feel Avery pressing her tender pussy against his manhood in reply. Looking down, he was even less surprised to find himself as taut and stiff as the wrought iron headboard she reached back and clung to as eagerly as he had only a few hours earlier.

"Speaking of coming to your senses, big guy," she murmured, grinding her swollen lips against his stiffening prick in a most suggestive manner. "This headboard's in desperate need of some hard, loud banging."

He shuddered pleasurably at the thought, gripping the rods on either side of her own hands as he pressed himself just inside her tempting pussy.

"Be careful what you wish for, hot pants."

Her breath was as hot and damp as her yielding crevice, whispering saucily against his earlobe. "Careful is the *last* thing I want to be right now, Branch Asher."

CHAPTER THIRTY-FIVE: AVERY

"Branch?"

Her voice just above a whisper, Avery struggled to rouse, thighs still quivering, and eyes swimming with the blurry visions of fleshy fantasy she'd just indulged in for the last few hours straight.

She lay still, letting the day greet her instead of rushing headfirst into the morn as she so often did. Gradually, moment by moment, breath by breath, Avery regained her senses. She didn't have to roll over to know Branch was out like a light, dead to the world. His flaring nostrils, noisy snoring, and the way his body was dead weight right next to her made that point perfectly clear.

"Baby?" she murmured anyway, half convinced they were telekinetically connected and that anytime she rose, an alarm went off somewhere deep inside, rousing him to drag her into his arms and seduce her in some strange, new, indulgent way.

But not this time. He was splayed out, tan skin bare and one ankle twisted in the damp, sodden bedsheets as, this time, his eyes remained shut—tight, and perhaps seeing the blur and flash of their fleshy fantasies merge to life behind those deeply shut eyelids.

She smirked, and gently so as not to rouse him—good Lord, she couldn't take another pounding like that one so soon—she slid from the bed, grabbed what clothes she could muster, and quietly slipped out of the bedroom.

Closing the door behind her, Avery sagged against the doorjamb and shimmied into her skirt and blouse, righting herself and looking for witnesses as if doing the walk-of-shame in her own living room.

Her own.

Living room.

She'd been so eager to share the news with Branch, Avery hadn't considered the long-range impact of her father's surprising—and surprisingly generous—gesture. Now, awakened from another post-coital cat nap, Avery marveled at the sudden turn of events as she brewed a pot of coffee and set about preparing a casual, rushed brunch for when Branch inevitably awoke.

As she waited, she blushed at what they'd already done, and even more brightly at what she still yearned to do. A week off before she started her new *job* at the warehouse. She hadn't had a week off since, well, she'd never had one, come to think of it. Avery had enrolled in college early, just after graduation, settling into her dorm room and classes before she'd barely had a chance to return her cap and gown.

Winter, summer, and spring breaks had been spent cramming for extra credit. And even after she earned her Bachelor's, she'd swept right into her master's program with barely a hitch between degrees.

Now, suddenly, back in her hometown, back in her old house, she felt freer than she had in years. No commitments, no deadlines, no pressure, no one to impress . . . for seven whole days. It was, indeed, an actual Christmas miracle. She poured a cup of coffee, stirring it with a peppermint stick and savoring the bittersweet brew as it roused her very soul.

Her cheery, jazzy, soulful holiday playlist had ended hours ago, filling the house with a silence she no longer craved. Suddenly, eagerly, she wanted voices. Loud, eager, playful, loving voices, the kind Branch had whenever they were together. The kind the kids at the warehouse had had, brainstorming under her slightly older, vaguely more experienced tutelage.

The yammering back and forth, good-natured ribbing, and simmering sarcasm the boys in the boardroom back at Balthazar Broadcasting had never quite mastered nor were tempted to enjoy.

Part of her simmering joy that early, bright, cheerful holiday morning was anticipation of another sort — a creative sort. The kind she'd never enjoyed while away at school and certainly not back in the home office. The kind of creativity and idea-generating energy she'd experienced at the warehouse.

She yearned to be part of something bigger than herself, to share a creative vision not just with Branch but with the energetic young team he'd assembled over the years. Her belly was taut with tension, the good type that came from positive stress and the eagerness to do a good job for a company, for a partner, she truly cared about.

But first?

Christmas, and lots of it.

She started the playlist over, humming gently along to the first tune as she topped off her coffee cup, grabbed a wholegrain croissant, and drifted casually toward the vast, long, low leather couch.

"Happy holidays," she murmured, joining her old partner Peggy Lee as she sipped and savored her morning brew in quiet contentment, the day stretching out before her like the soft tendrils of steam quietly escaping her sedate gray coffee mug.

Happy she was, indeed.

Finally, firmly, indubitably happy.

She gently wriggled deeper into her seat, naked beneath her thin, crinkly skirt, thrilled at the sounds of stirring behind the bedroom door. The snoring had stopped, and plaintively, distantly, she heard Branch calling her name as he roused from the squeaky, tortured mattress.

She set the coffee cup down, swallowed her croissant, and

waited, a fresh fantasy brewing as bubbly and hot and fragrant as the morning coffee just had.

"Happy holidays," she murmured anew, deep-throated and belly taut as the door opened and Branch stood, buff and bare and long and lean and judging from his, uh, excitement, more than ready to greet the day with a fresh and tasty fantasy.

A Christmas fantasy, just for them . . .

ABOUT THE AUTHOR

Alex Winters is the pseudonym of a busy restaurant manager whose curious young staff would love nothing more than to follow him around the dining room reading his steamiest, most romantic passages aloud! When not writing romantic holiday stories of various heat levels, he enjoys long walks with his wife, scary movies and smooth jazz. Visit him at his website to see what stories are brewing up next!